D1539266

THE **HORSE-RIDING** ADVENTURE OF **SYBIL LUDINGTON,**

REVOLUTIONARY WAR MESSENGER

BY **MARSHA AMSTEL**
ADAPTED BY **AMANDA DOERING TOURVILLE**
ILLUSTRATED BY **TED HAMMOND** AND **RICHARD PIMENTEL CARBAJAL**

Graphic Universe™ Minneapolis • New York

INTRODUCTION

IN THE 1600S, GREAT BRITAIN BEGAN SETTING UP COLONIES IN NORTH AMERICA. EVENTUALLY, THERE WERE 13 OF THEM. BY 1775, MANY AMERICANS HAD BECOME IMPATIENT WITH BEING PART OF BRITAIN. THEY WANTED THEIR OWN GOVERNMENT. THEY WANTED TO MAKE LAWS AND SOLVE PROBLEMS ON THEIR OWN. THEY WANTED TO BE A FREE AND INDEPENDENT NATION. BUT BRITAIN HAD NO INTENTION OF LETTING ITS COLONIES GO FREE.

MANY BRITISH SOLDIERS CAME ON SHIPS TO BOSTON IN THE COLONY OF MASSACHUSETTS. AMERICANS THROUGHOUT THE COLONIES BEGAN TO PREPARE FOR WAR. AMERICANS FOUGHT BRITISH SOLDIERS AT THE BATTLE OF LEXINGTON ON APRIL 19, 1775. THIS WAS THE BEGINNING OF THE REVOLUTIONARY WAR (1775-1783).

THE REVOLUTIONARY WAR CONTINUED FOR YEARS. MANY AMERICANS WHO FOUGHT IN THE WAR WERE NOT FULL-TIME SOLDIERS. THEY WERE FARMERS AND CRAFTSPEOPLE, AND THEY WORKED IN THEIR FIELDS AND SHOPS UNTIL THEY WERE CALLED UPON TO FIGHT. THEY WERE KNOWN AS MILITIA.

HENRY LUDINGTON WAS A FARMER AND MILL OWNER IN PATTERSON, NEW YORK. HE LIVED WITH HIS WIFE AND EIGHT CHILDREN. HIS ELDEST, SYBIL, WAS 16. LUDINGTON LED A GROUP OF MILITIA. AFTER MONTHS OF FIGHTING, COLONEL LUDINGTON AND HIS MEN RETURNED TO THEIR FARMS SO THAT THEY COULD PLANT THEIR SPRING CROPS. ON APRIL 25, 1777, HIS SOLDIERS WERE AT HOME WITH THEIR FAMILIES. BUT A NEW THREAT WAS APPROACHING THE COASTLINE OF NEARBY CONNECTICUT, AND YOUNG SYBIL WOULD SOON HAVE AN IMPORTANT PART TO PLAY IN THE CONFLICT.

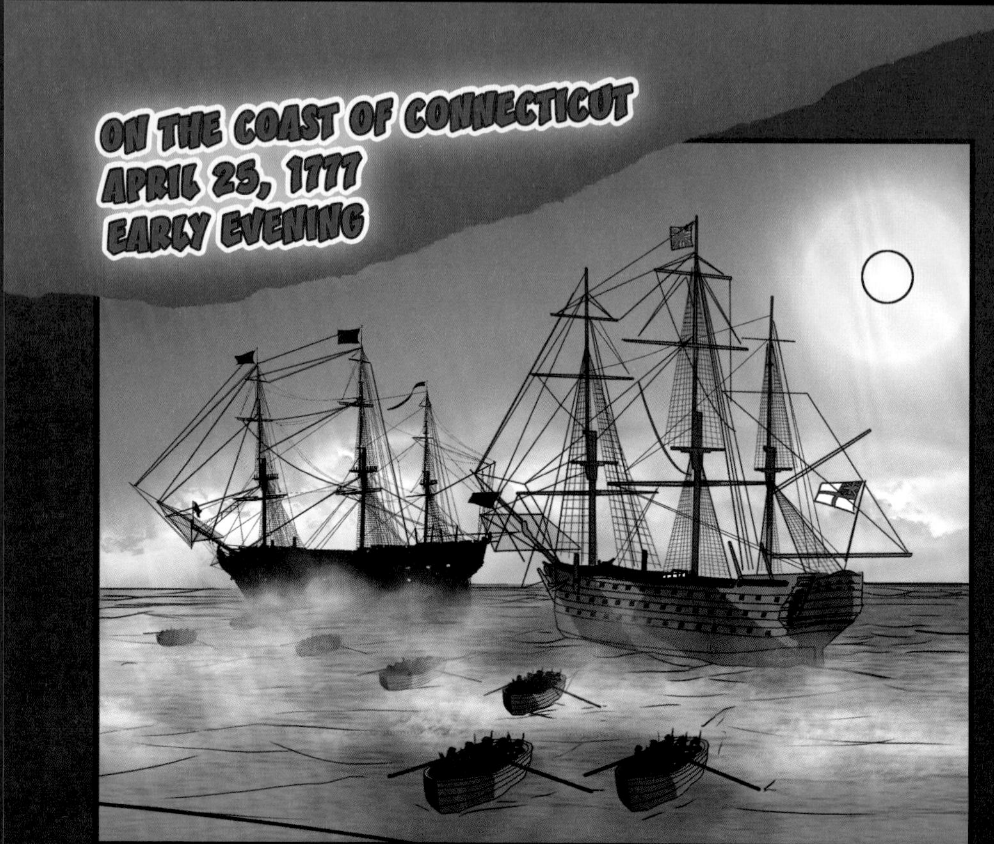
ON THE COAST OF CONNECTICUT
APRIL 25, 1777
EARLY EVENING

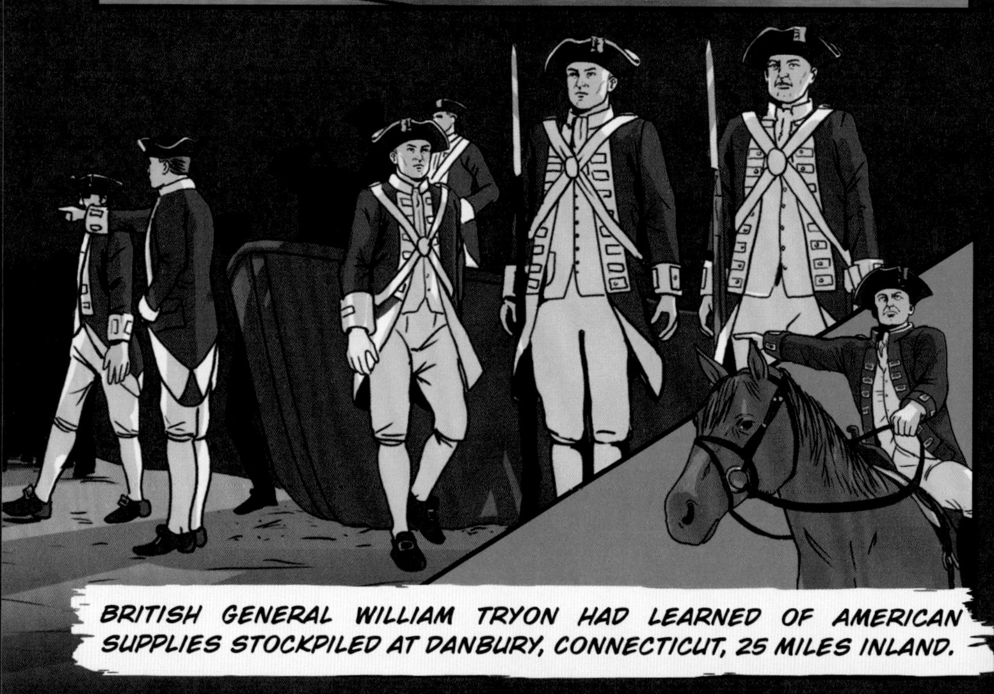
BRITISH GENERAL WILLIAM TRYON HAD LEARNED OF AMERICAN SUPPLIES STOCKPILED AT DANBURY, CONNECTICUT, 25 MILES INLAND.

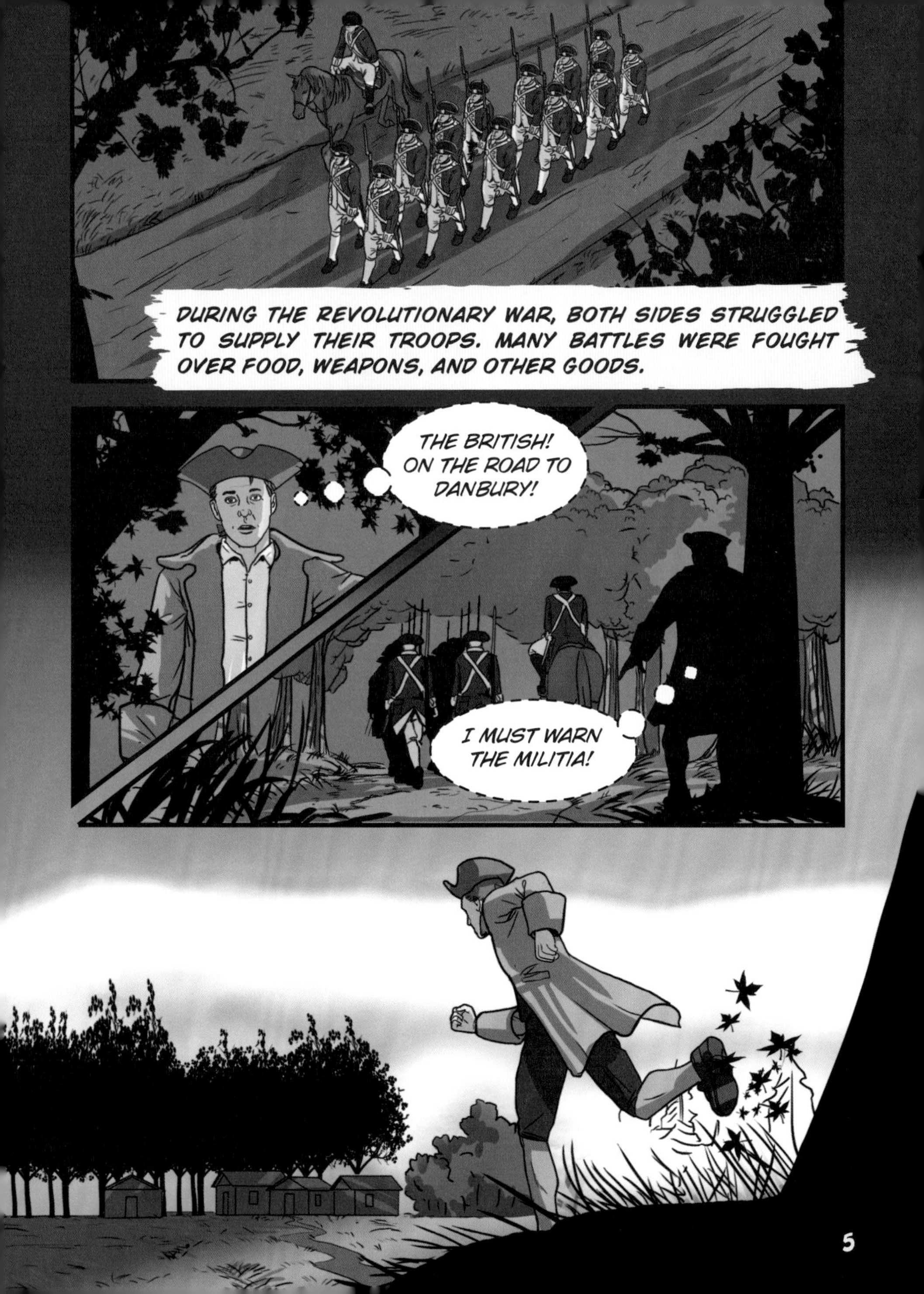
DURING THE REVOLUTIONARY WAR, BOTH SIDES STRUGGLED TO SUPPLY THEIR TROOPS. MANY BATTLES WERE FOUGHT OVER FOOD, WEAPONS, AND OTHER GOODS.
THE BRITISH! ON THE ROAD TO DANBURY!
I MUST WARN THE MILITIA!

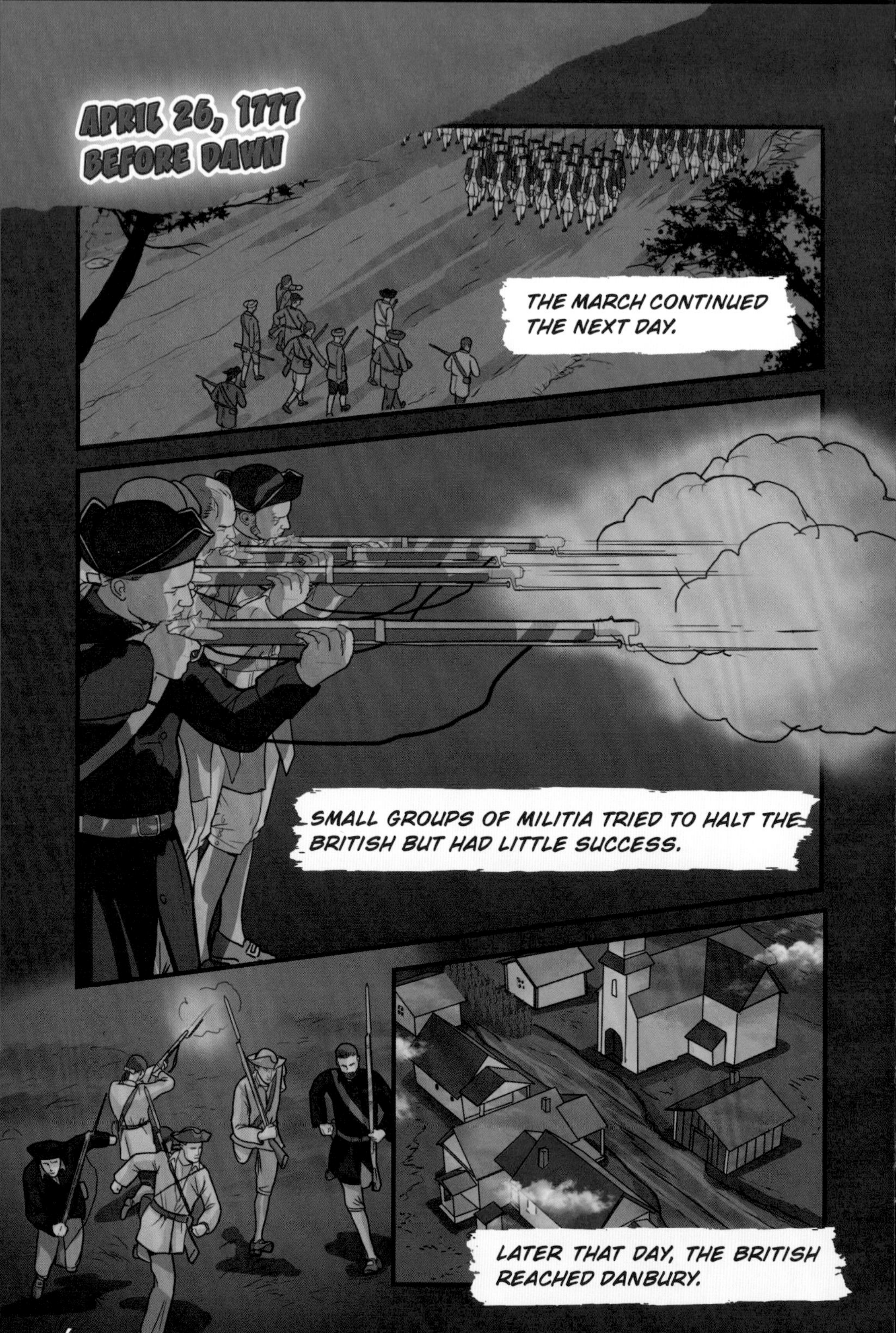
APRIL 26, 1777
BEFORE DAWN
THE MARCH CONTINUED THE NEXT DAY.
SMALL GROUPS OF MILITIA TRIED TO HALT THE BRITISH BUT HAD LITTLE SUCCESS.
LATER THAT DAY, THE BRITISH REACHED DANBURY.

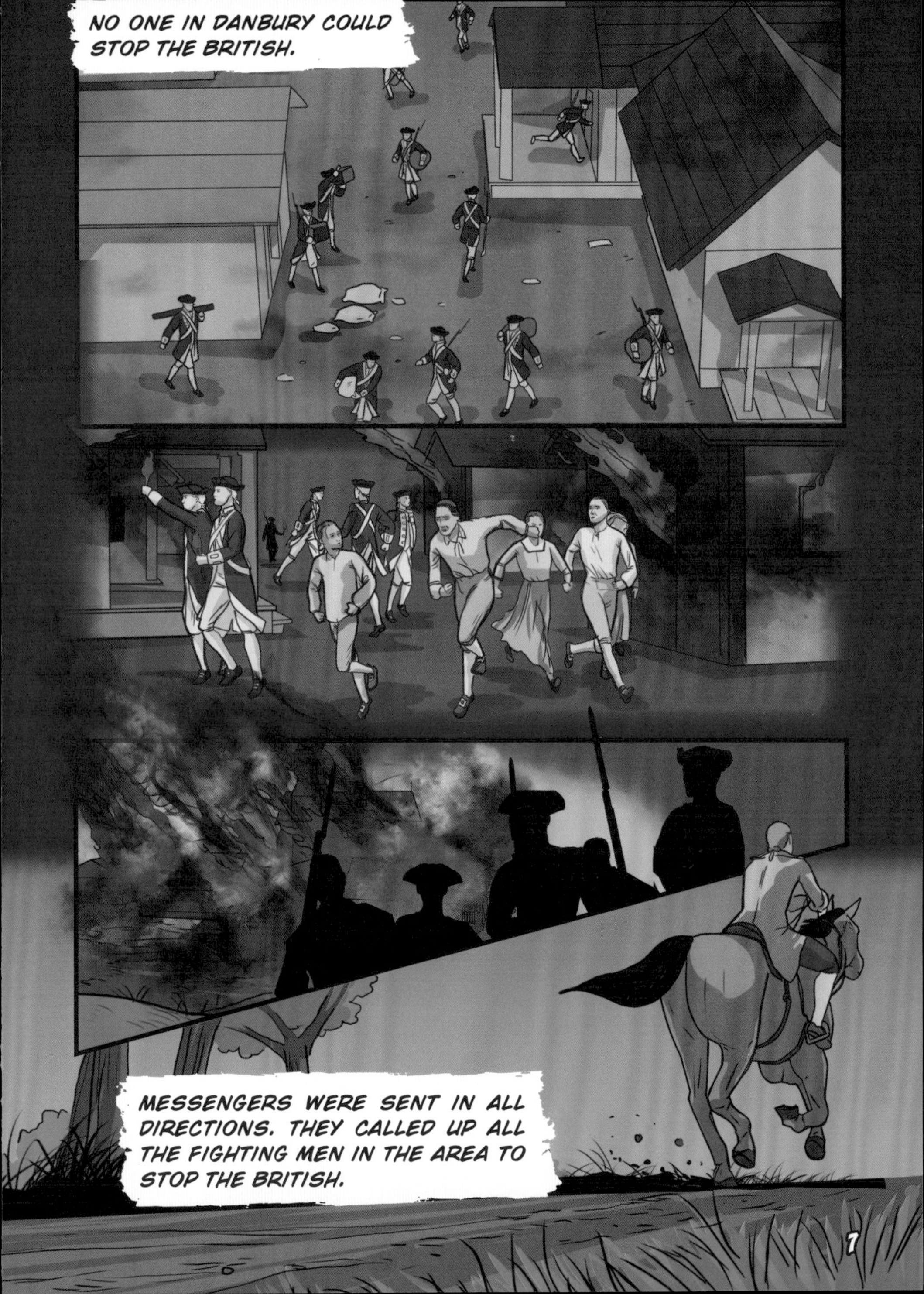
NO ONE IN DANBURY COULD STOP THE BRITISH.
MESSENGERS WERE SENT IN ALL DIRECTIONS. THEY CALLED UP ALL THE FIGHTING MEN IN THE AREA TO STOP THE BRITISH.

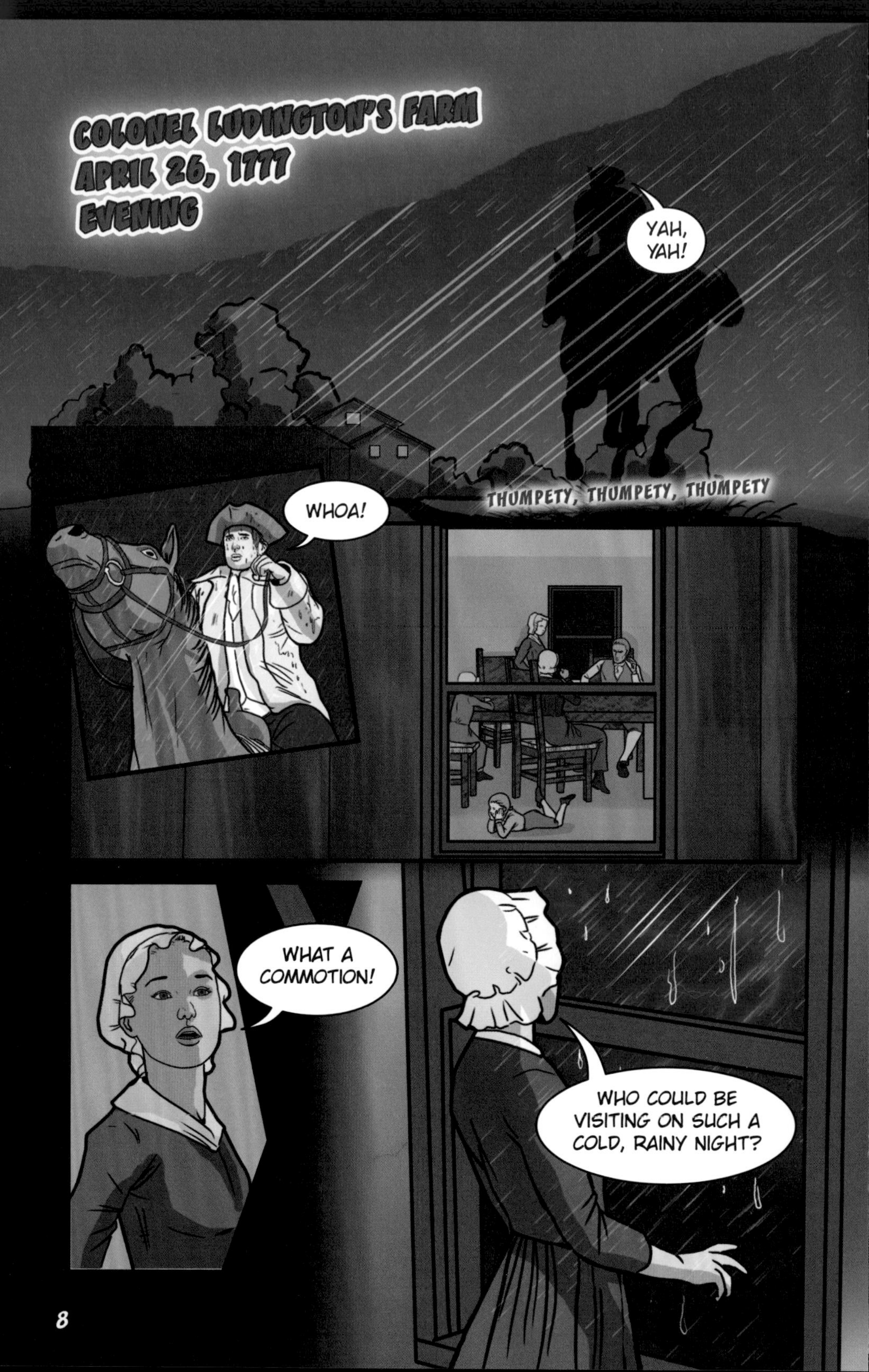
COLONEL LUDINGTON'S FARM
APRIL 26, 1777
EVENING
YAH, YAH!
THUMPETY, THUMPETY, THUMPETY
WHOA!
WHAT A COMMOTION!
WHO COULD BE VISITING ON SUCH A COLD, RAINY NIGHT?

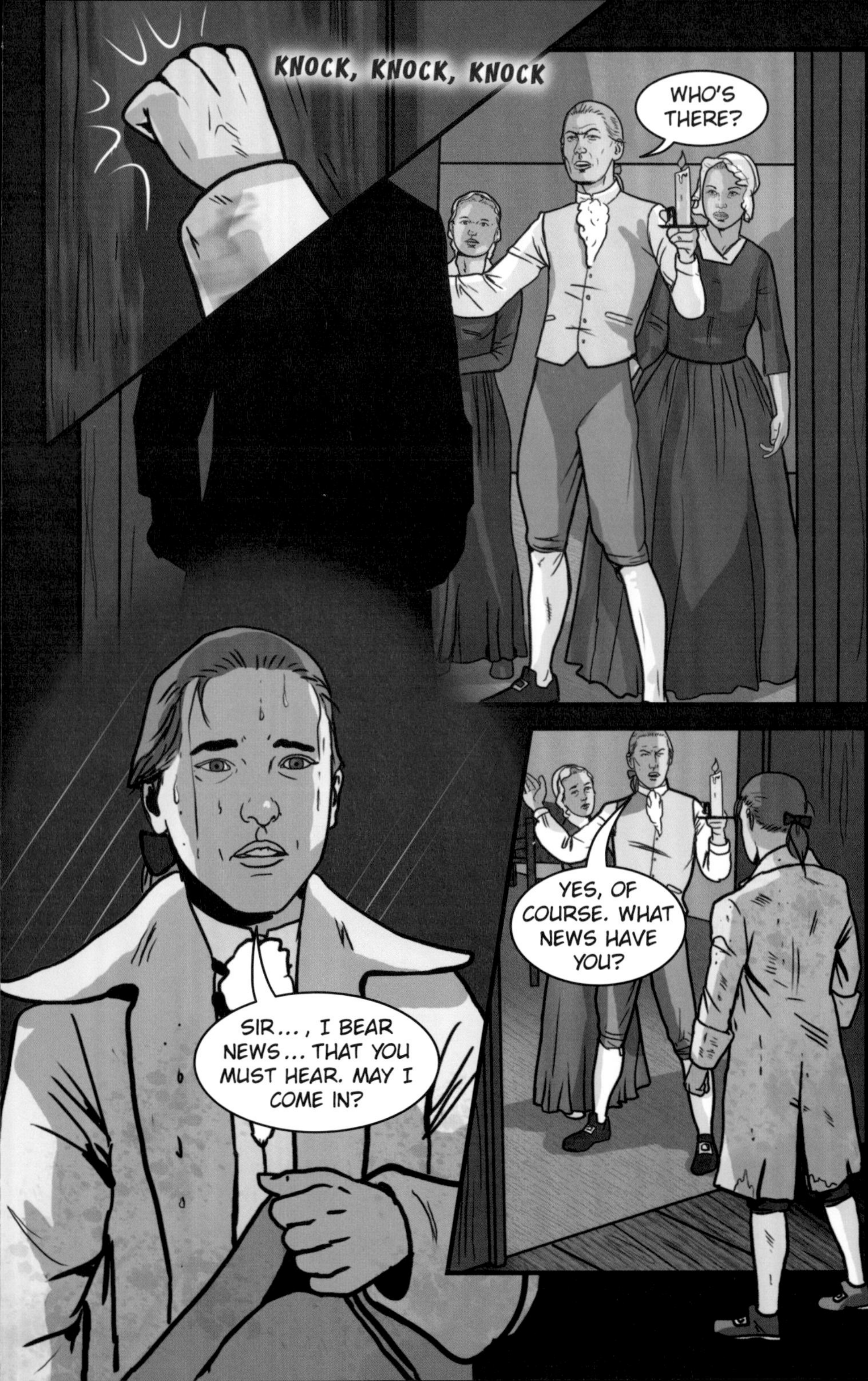
KNOCK, KNOCK, KNOCK
WHO'S THERE?
SIR..., I BEAR NEWS... THAT YOU MUST HEAR. MAY I COME IN?
YES, OF COURSE. WHAT NEWS HAVE YOU?

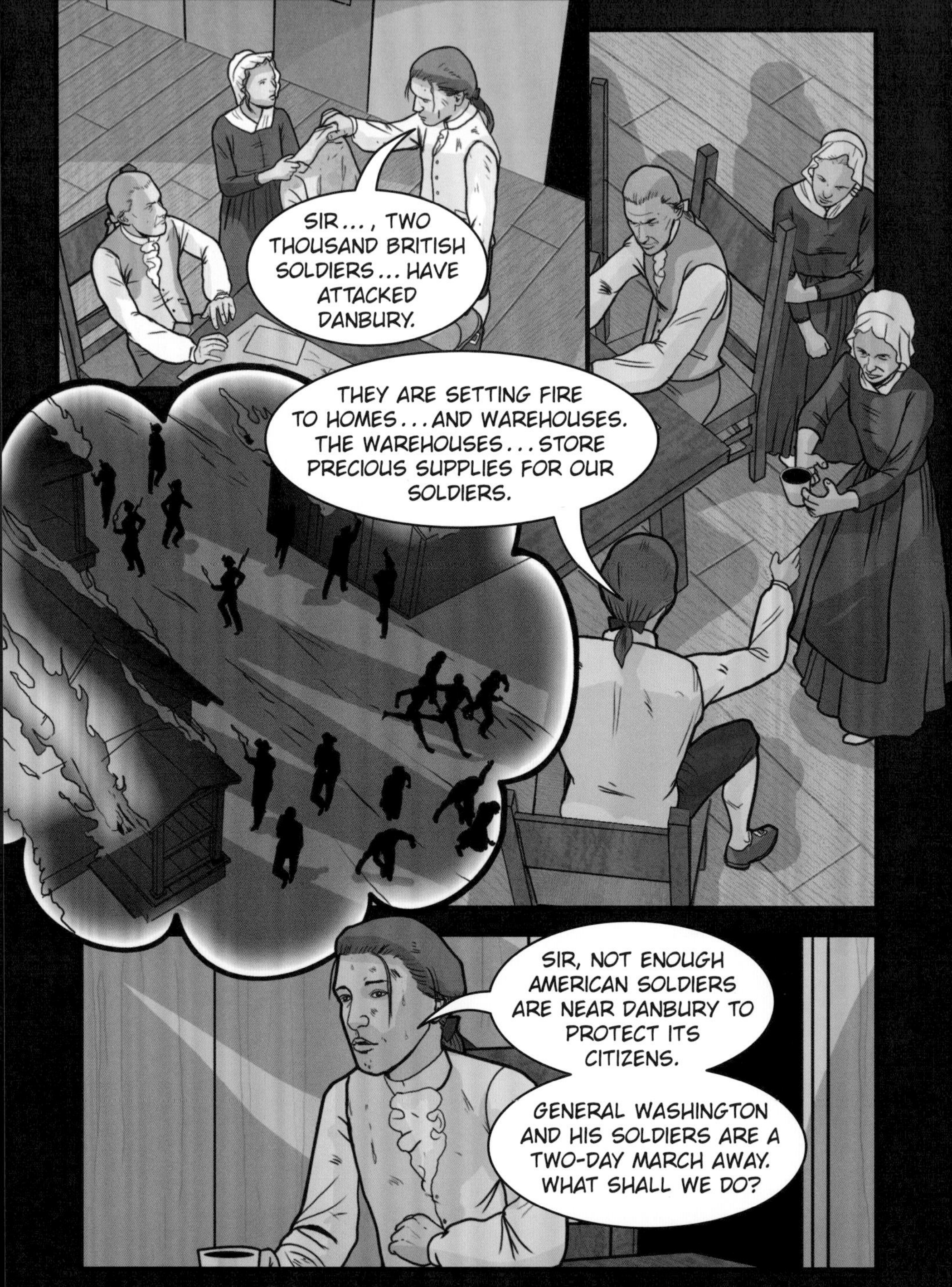
SIR..., TWO THOUSAND BRITISH SOLDIERS... HAVE ATTACKED DANBURY.
THEY ARE SETTING FIRE TO HOMES...AND WAREHOUSES. THE WAREHOUSES...STORE PRECIOUS SUPPLIES FOR OUR SOLDIERS.
SIR, NOT ENOUGH AMERICAN SOLDIERS ARE NEAR DANBURY TO PROTECT ITS CITIZENS.
GENERAL WASHINGTON AND HIS SOLDIERS ARE A TWO-DAY MARCH AWAY. WHAT SHALL WE DO?

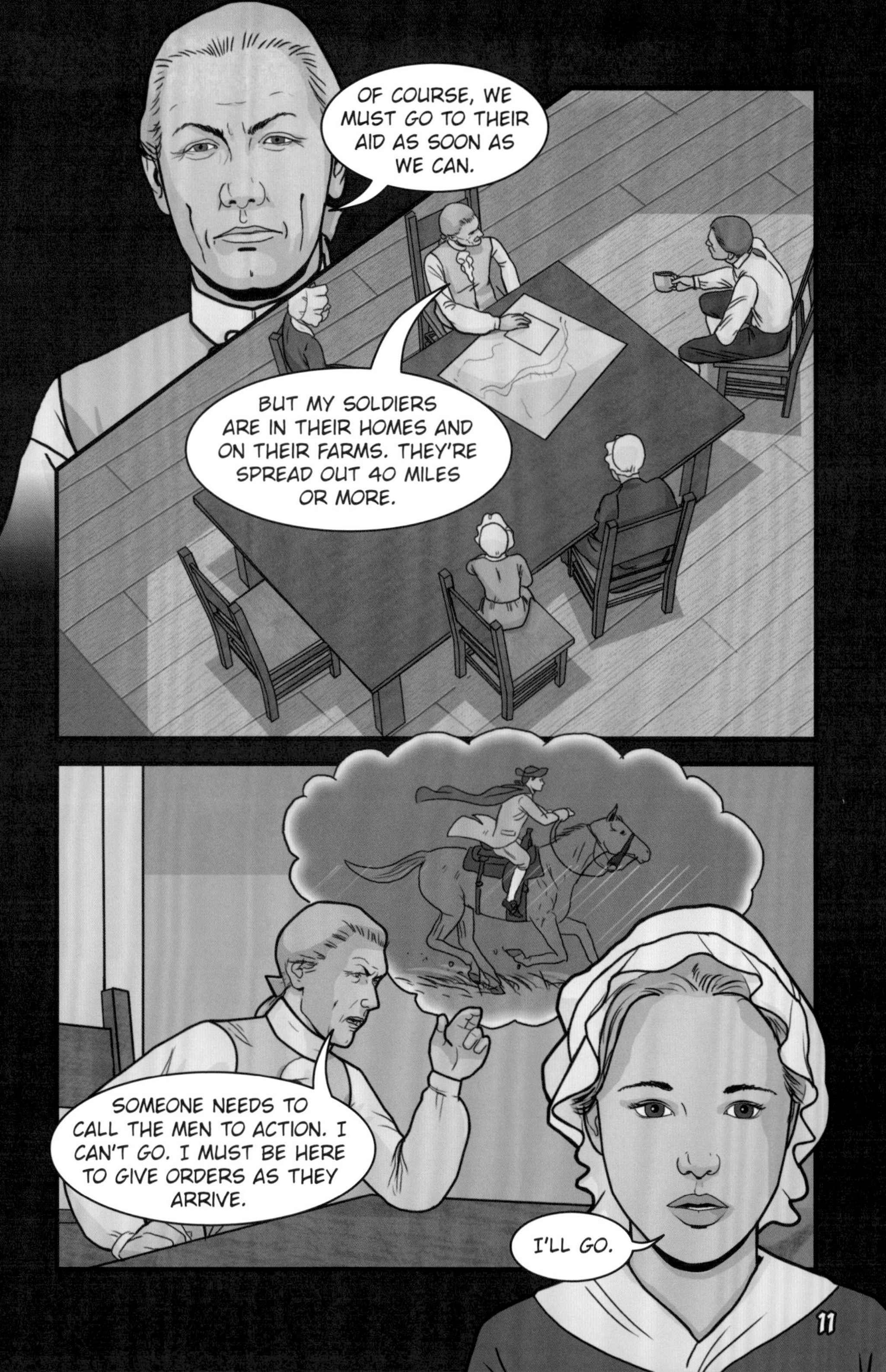
OF COURSE, WE MUST GO TO THEIR AID AS SOON AS WE CAN.
BUT MY SOLDIERS ARE IN THEIR HOMES AND ON THEIR FARMS. THEY'RE SPREAD OUT 40 MILES OR MORE.
SOMEONE NEEDS TO CALL THE MEN TO ACTION. I CAN'T GO. I MUST BE HERE TO GIVE ORDERS AS THEY ARRIVE.
I'LL GO.

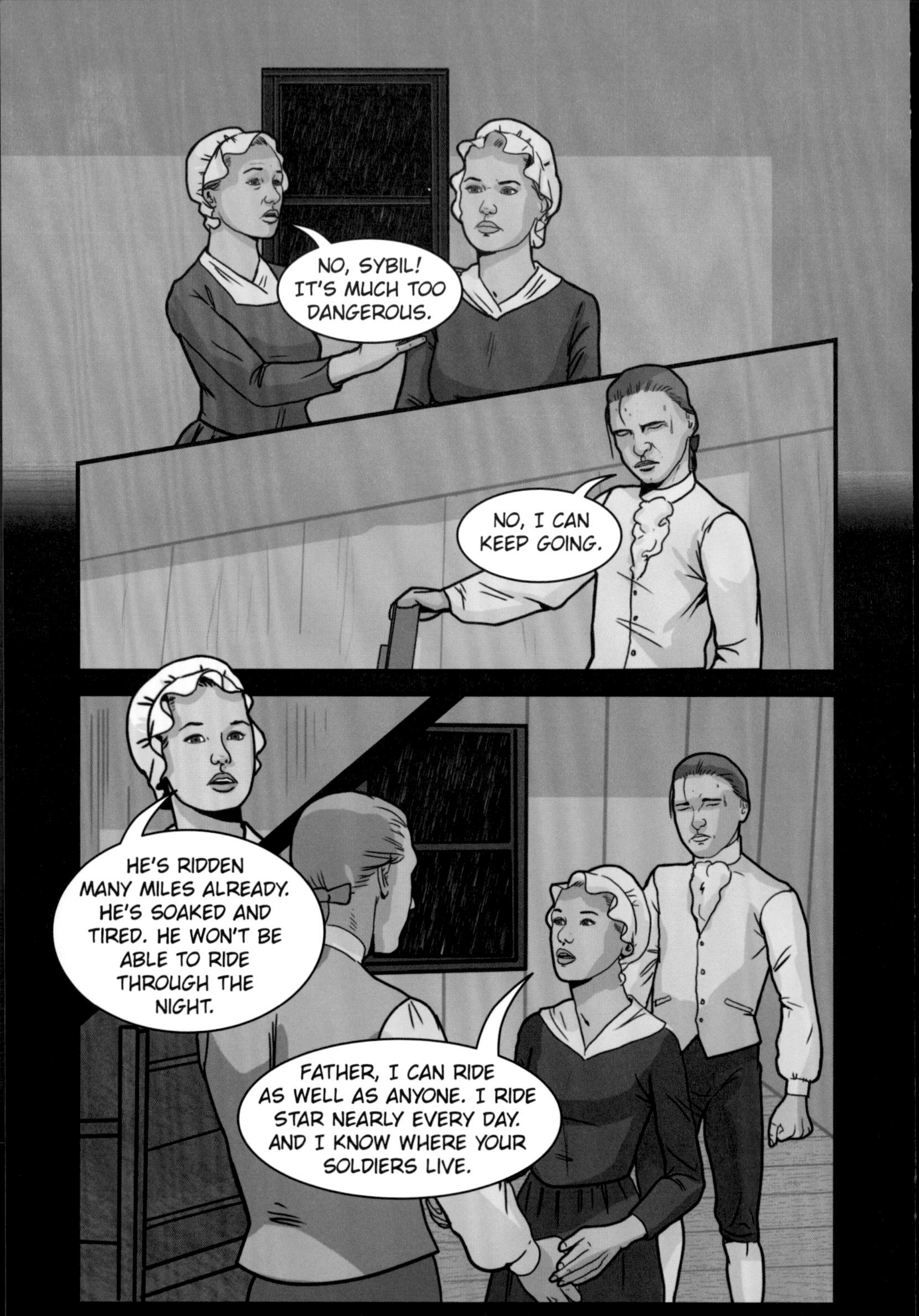
NO, SYBIL! IT'S MUCH TOO DANGEROUS.
NO, I CAN KEEP GOING.
HE'S RIDDEN MANY MILES ALREADY. HE'S SOAKED AND TIRED. HE WON'T BE ABLE TO RIDE THROUGH THE NIGHT.
FATHER, I CAN RIDE AS WELL AS ANYONE. I RIDE STAR NEARLY EVERY DAY. AND I KNOW WHERE YOUR SOLDIERS LIVE.

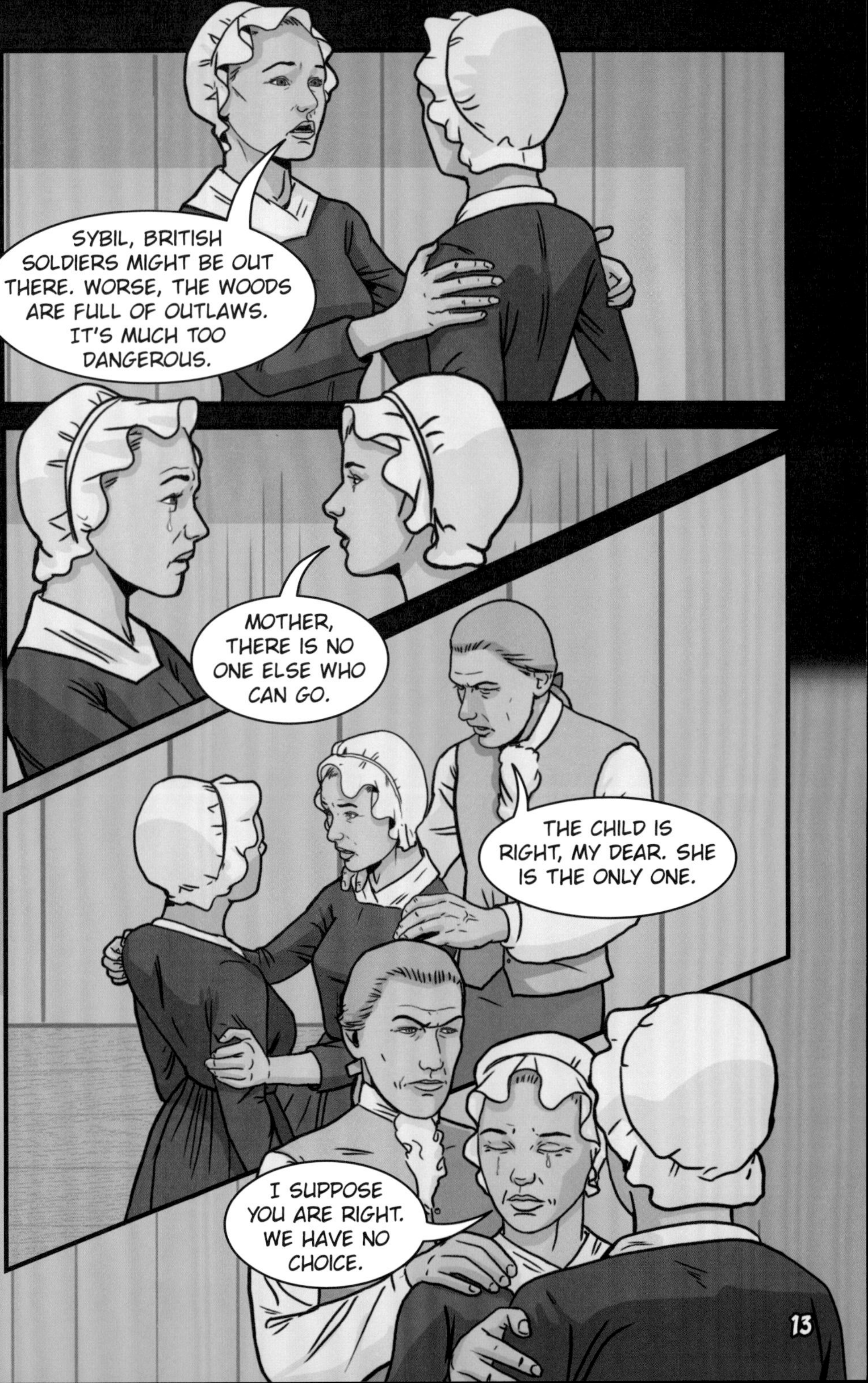
SYBIL, BRITISH SOLDIERS MIGHT BE OUT THERE. WORSE, THE WOODS ARE FULL OF OUTLAWS. IT'S MUCH TOO DANGEROUS.
MOTHER, THERE IS NO ONE ELSE WHO CAN GO.
THE CHILD IS RIGHT, MY DEAR. SHE IS THE ONLY ONE.
I SUPPOSE YOU ARE RIGHT. WE HAVE NO CHOICE.

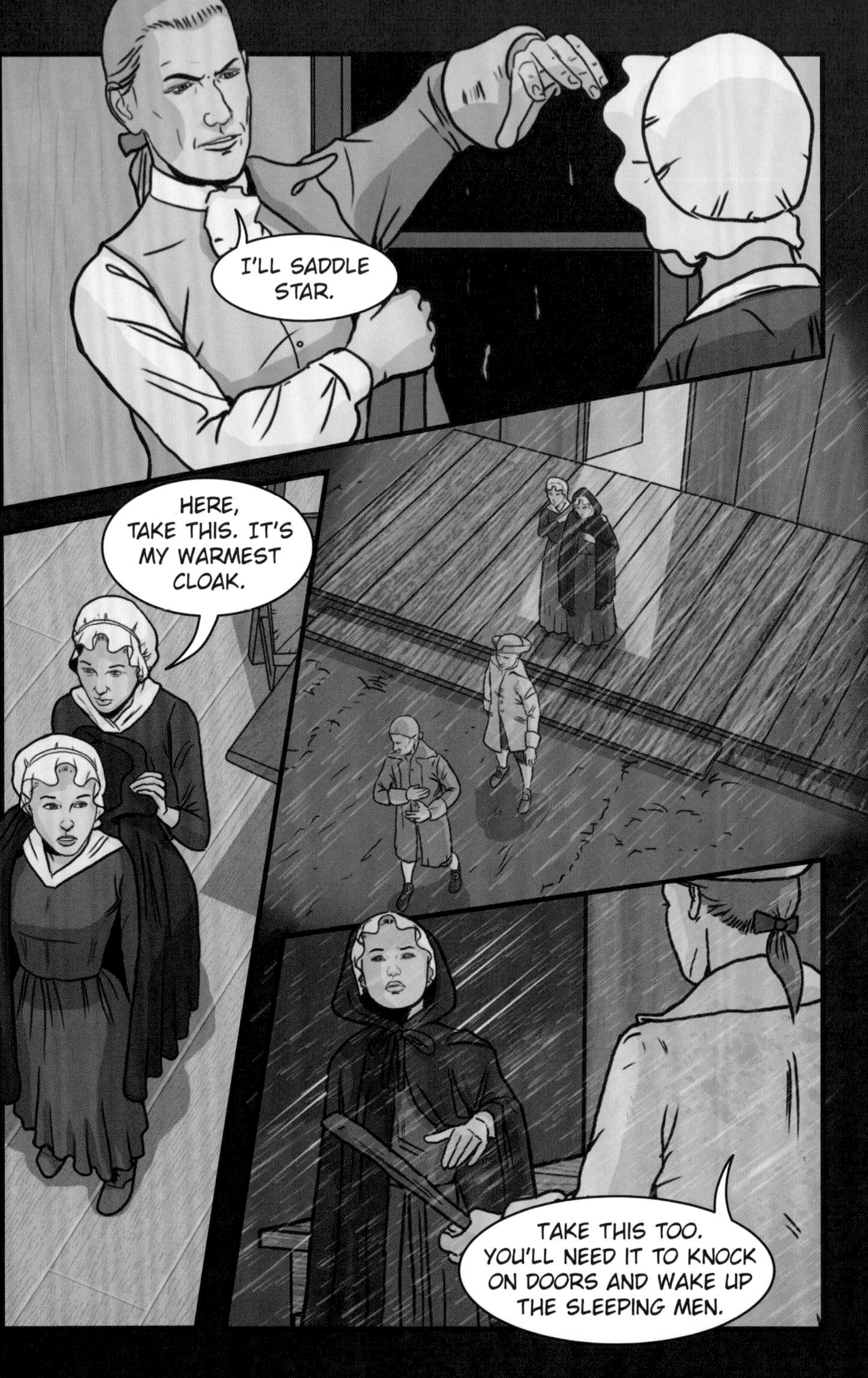
I'LL SADDLE STAR.
HERE, TAKE THIS. IT'S MY WARMEST CLOAK.
TAKE THIS TOO. YOU'LL NEED IT TO KNOCK ON DOORS AND WAKE UP THE SLEEPING MEN.

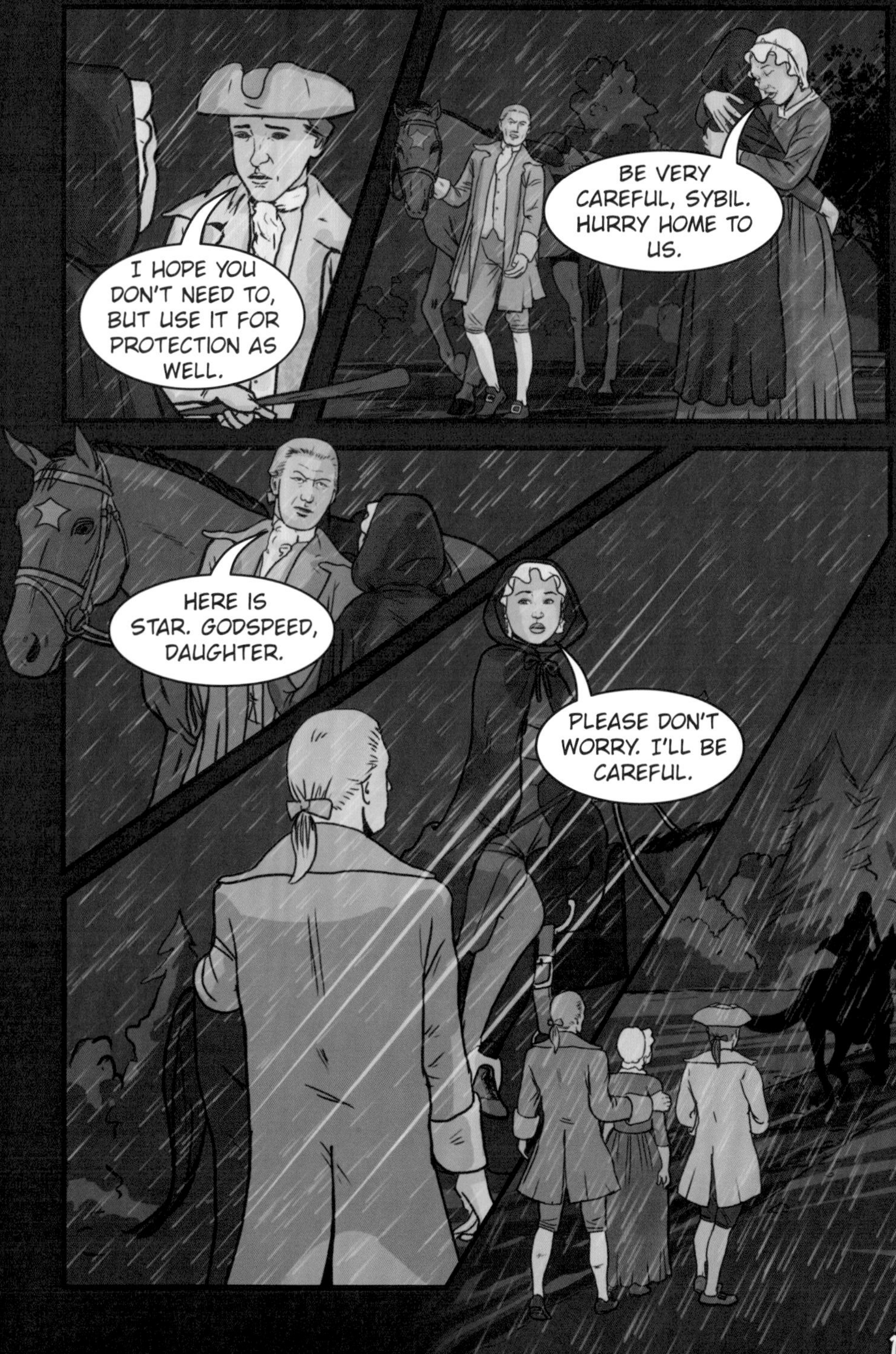
I HOPE YOU DON'T NEED TO, BUT USE IT FOR PROTECTION AS WELL.
BE VERY CAREFUL, SYBIL. HURRY HOME TO US.
HERE IS STAR. GODSPEED, DAUGHTER.
PLEASE DON'T WORRY. I'LL BE CAREFUL.

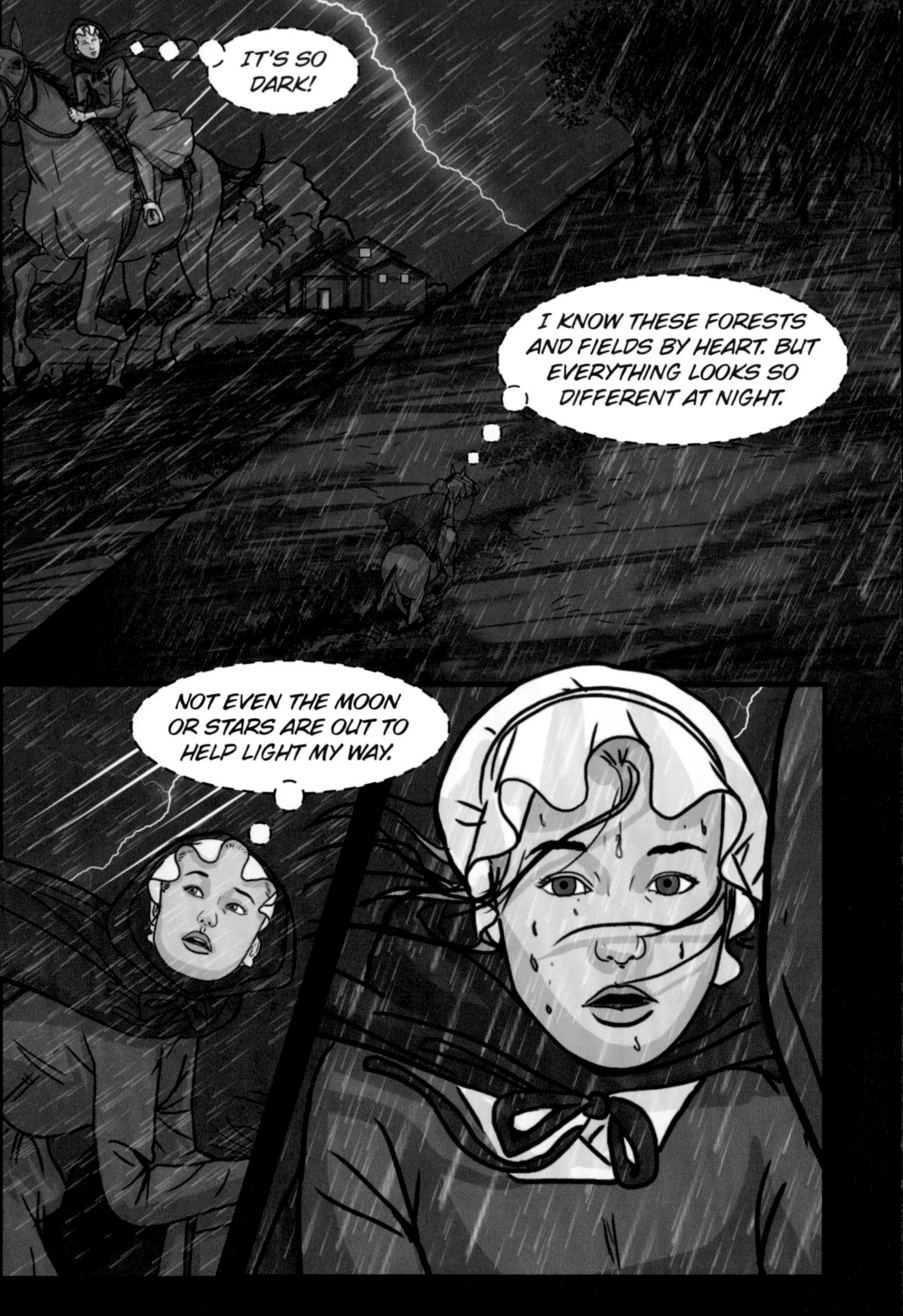
IT'S SO DARK!
I KNOW THESE FORESTS AND FIELDS BY HEART. BUT EVERYTHING LOOKS SO DIFFERENT AT NIGHT.
NOT EVEN THE MOON OR STARS ARE OUT TO HELP LIGHT MY WAY.

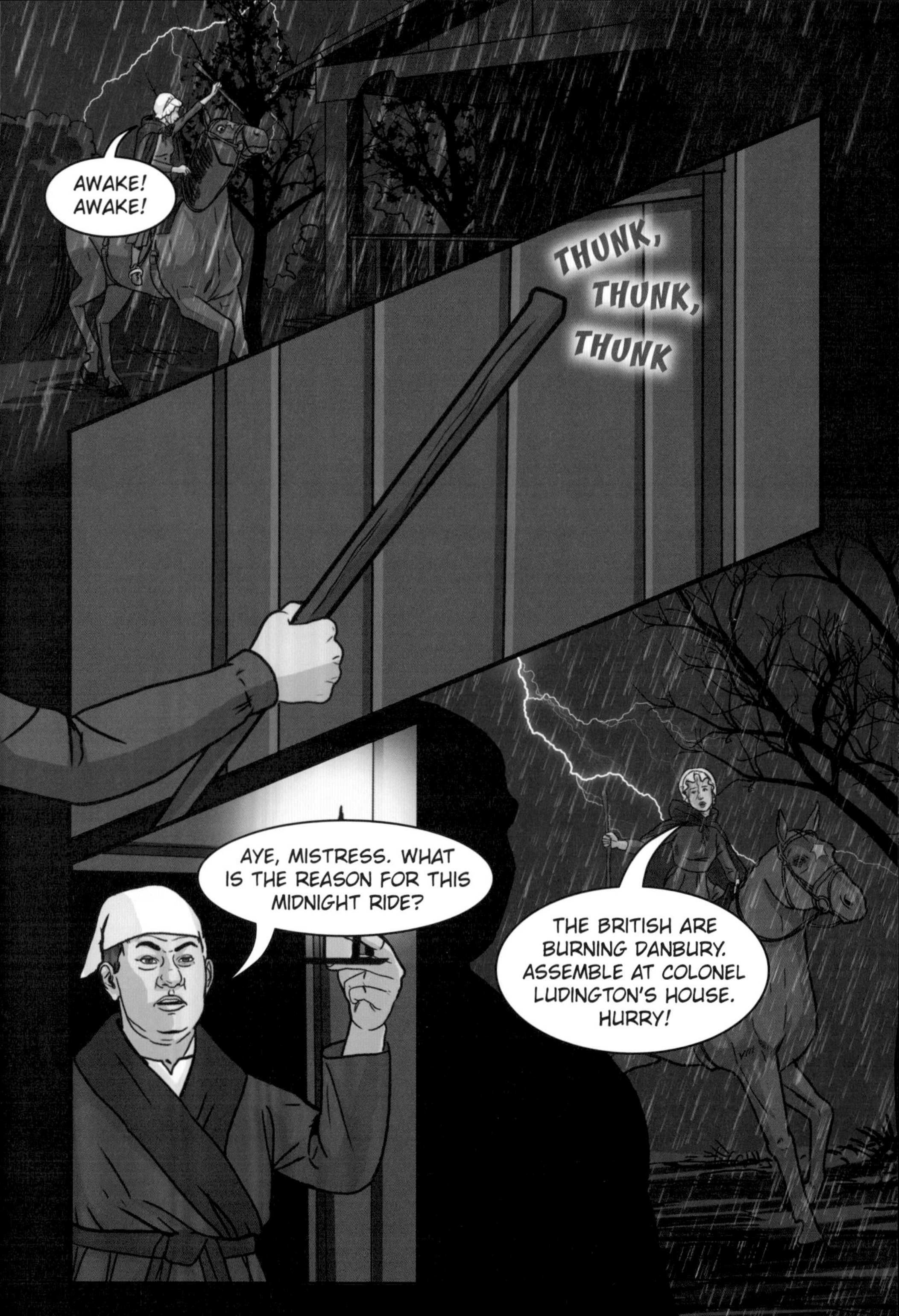
AWAKE! AWAKE!
THUNK, THUNK, THUNK
AYE, MISTRESS. WHAT IS THE REASON FOR THIS MIDNIGHT RIDE?
THE BRITISH ARE BURNING DANBURY. ASSEMBLE AT COLONEL LUDINGTON'S HOUSE. HURRY!

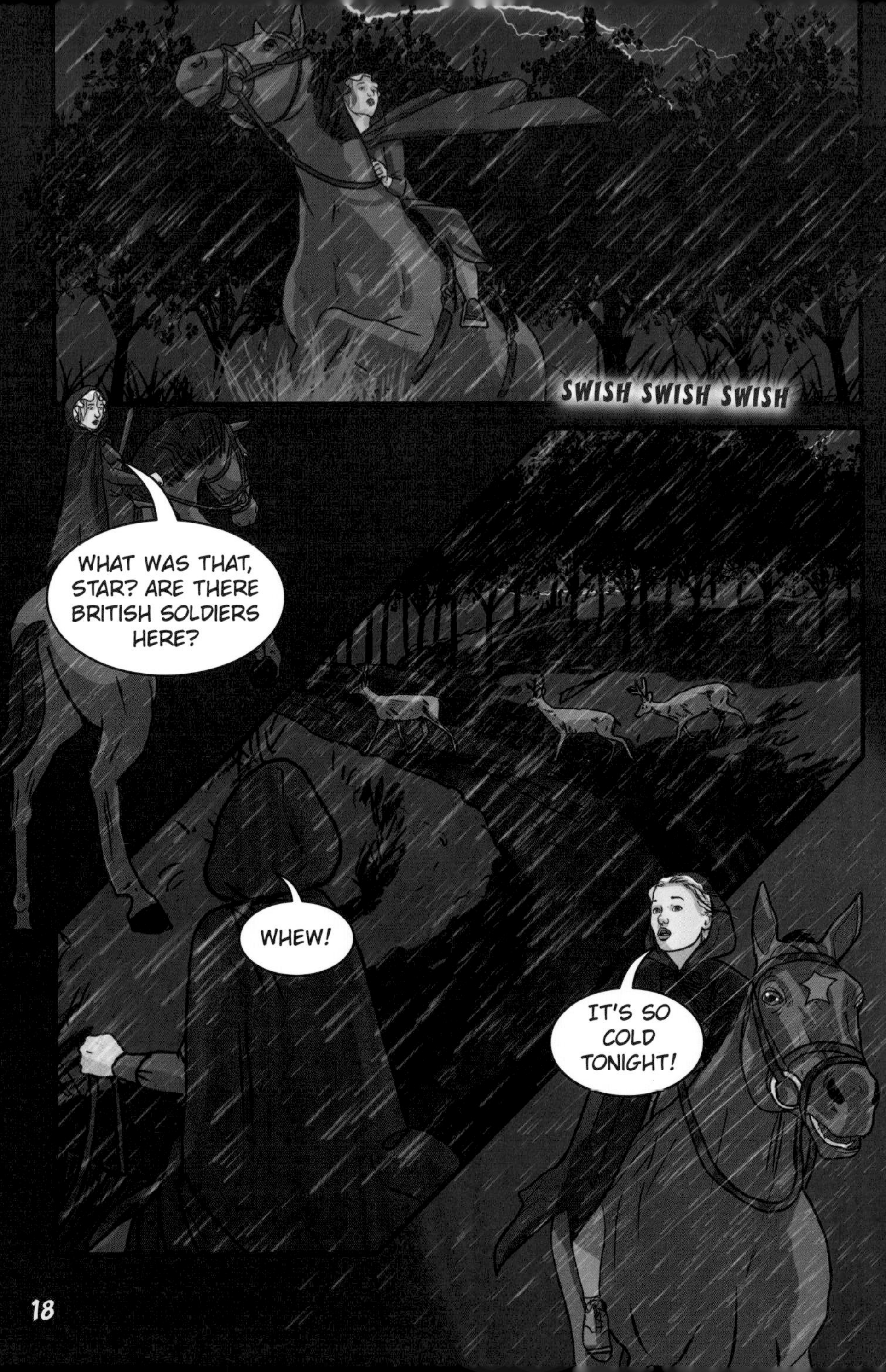
SWISH SWISH SWISH
WHAT WAS THAT, STAR? ARE THERE BRITISH SOLDIERS HERE?
WHEW!
IT'S SO COLD TONIGHT!

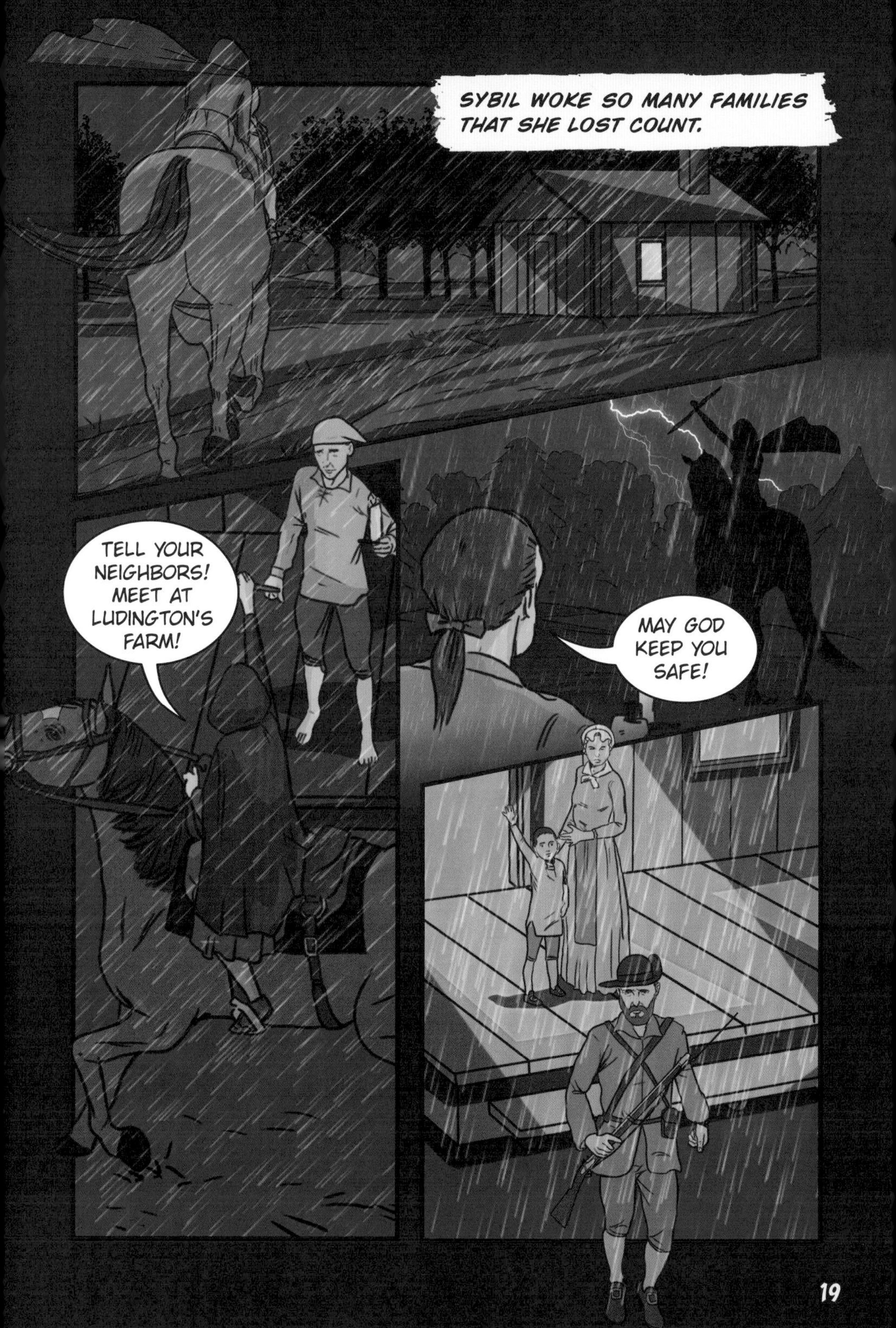
SYBIL WOKE SO MANY FAMILIES THAT SHE LOST COUNT.
TELL YOUR NEIGHBORS! MEET AT LUDINGTON'S FARM!
MAY GOD KEEP YOU SAFE!

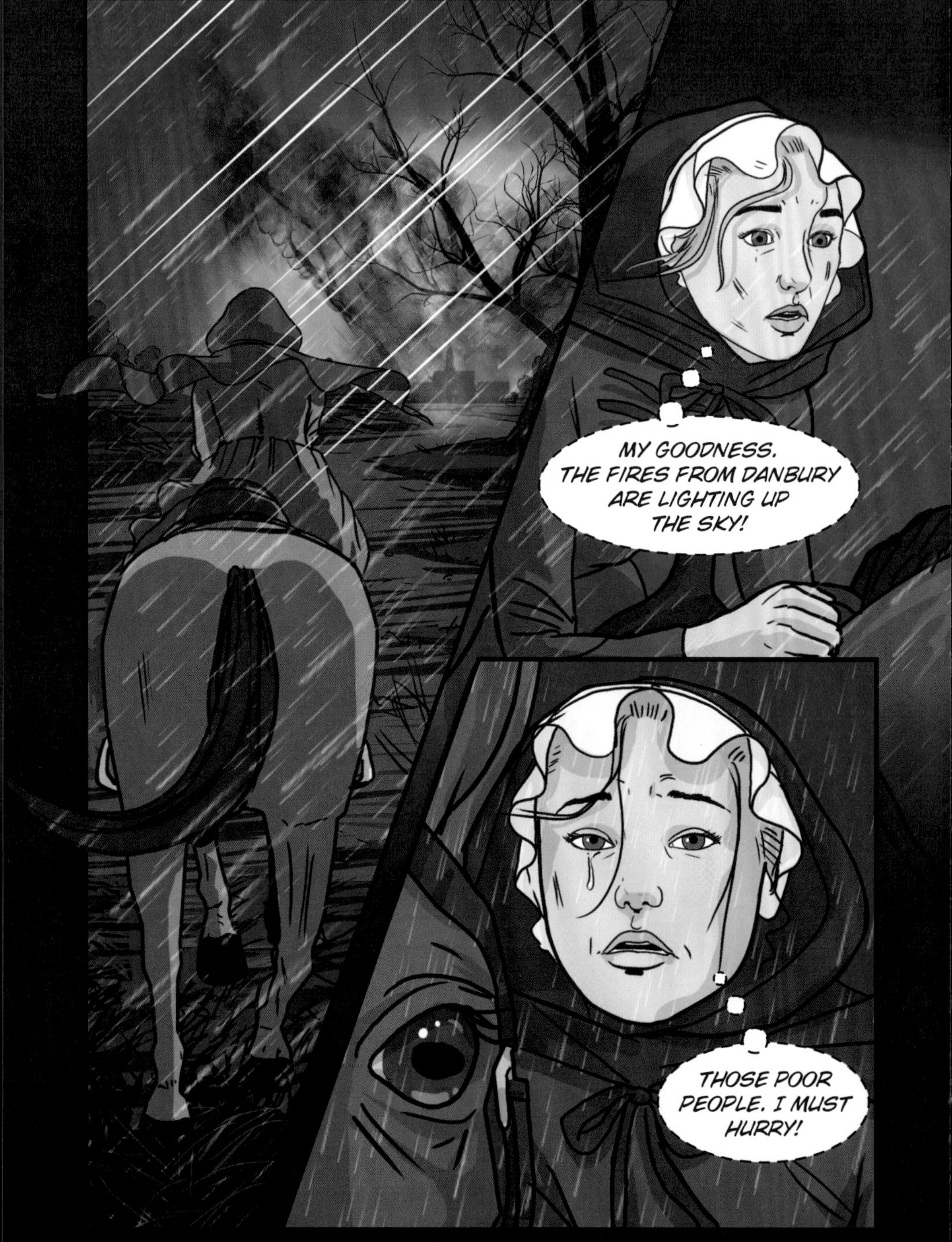
MY GOODNESS. THE FIRES FROM DANBURY ARE LIGHTING UP THE SKY!
THOSE POOR PEOPLE. I MUST HURRY!

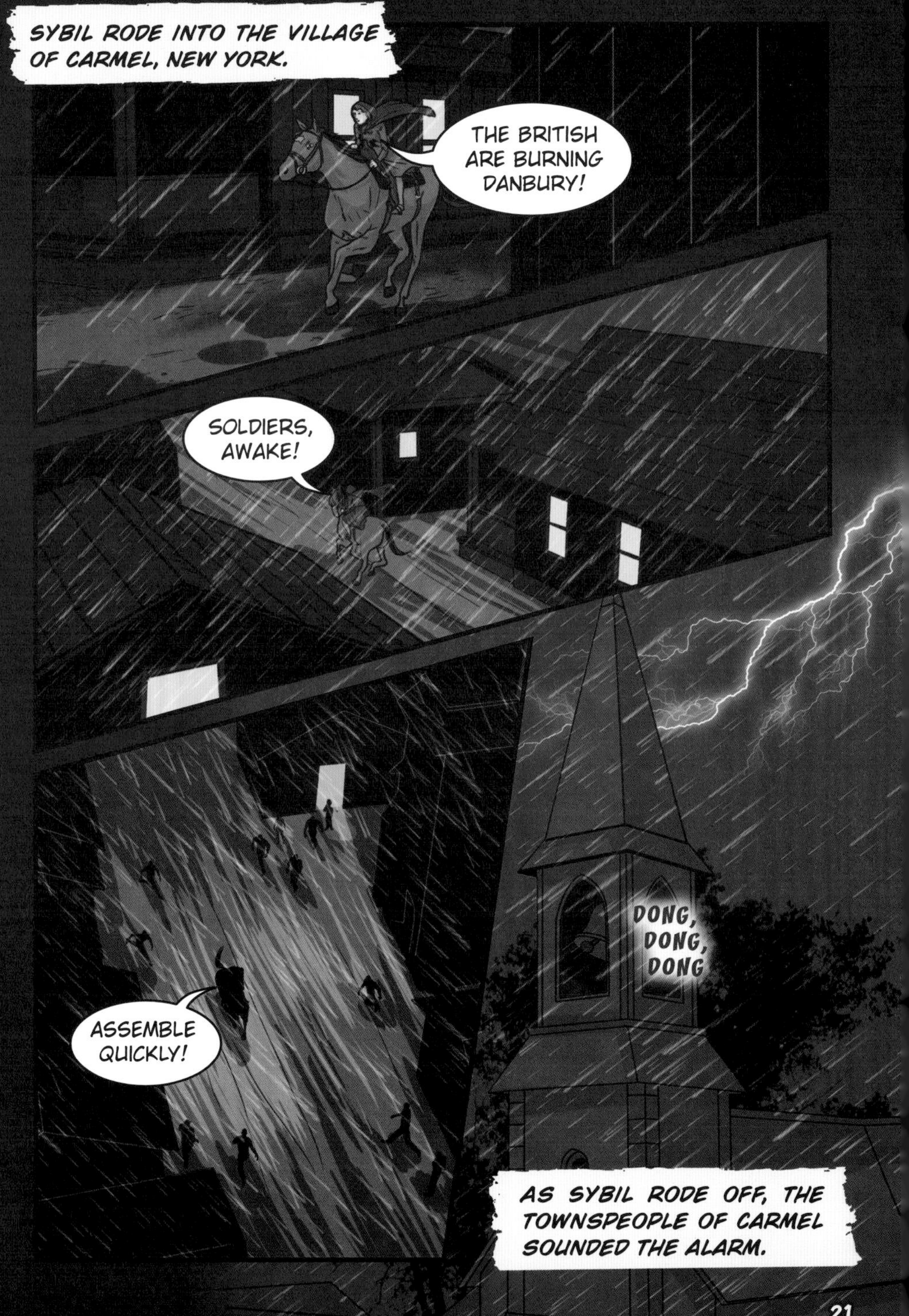
SYBIL RODE INTO THE VILLAGE OF CARMEL, NEW YORK.
THE BRITISH ARE BURNING DANBURY!
SOLDIERS, AWAKE!
ASSEMBLE QUICKLY!
DONG, DONG, DONG
AS SYBIL RODE OFF, THE TOWNSPEOPLE OF CARMEL SOUNDED THE ALARM.

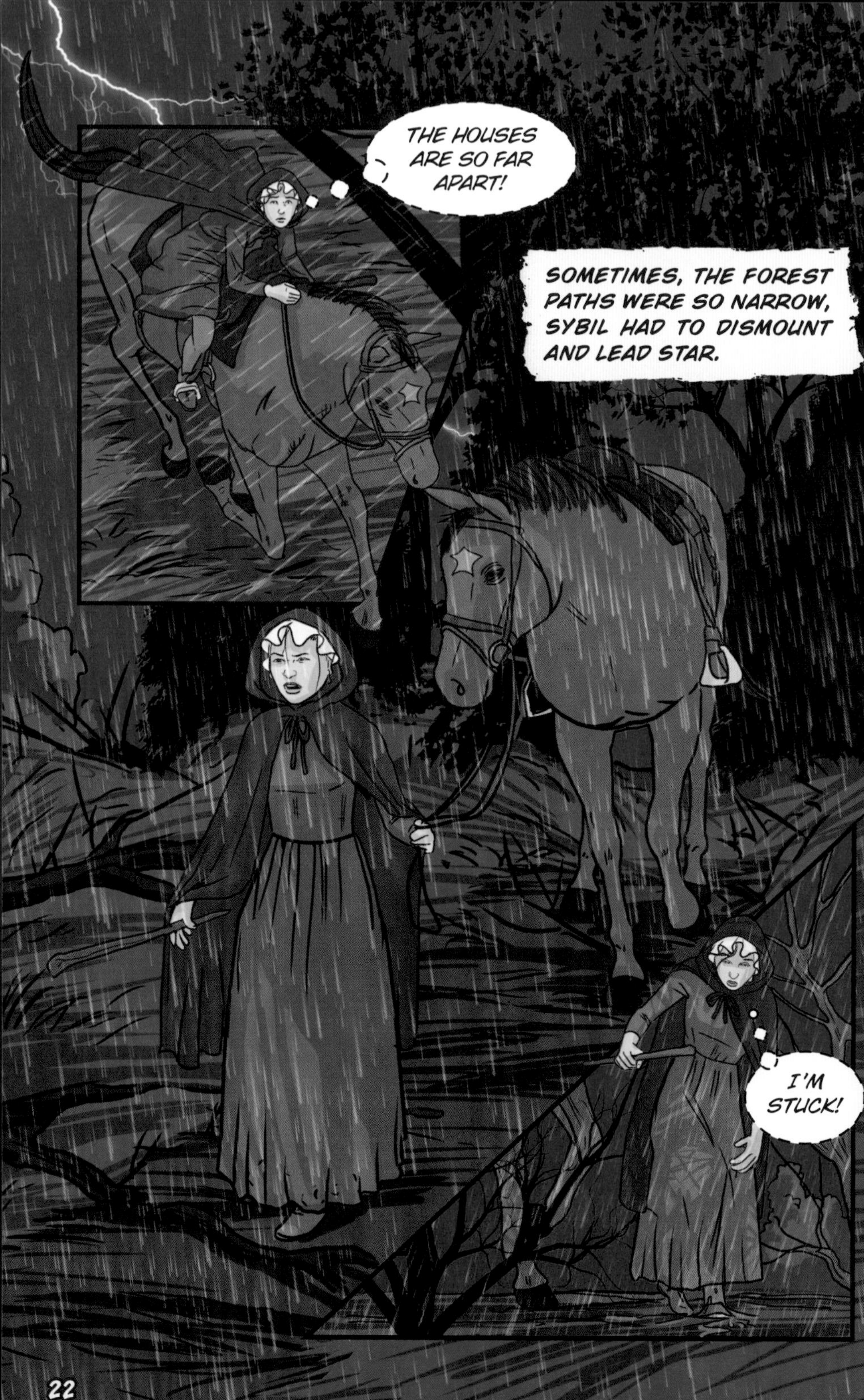
THE HOUSES ARE SO FAR APART!
SOMETIMES, THE FOREST PATHS WERE SO NARROW, SYBIL HAD TO DISMOUNT AND LEAD STAR.
I'M STUCK!

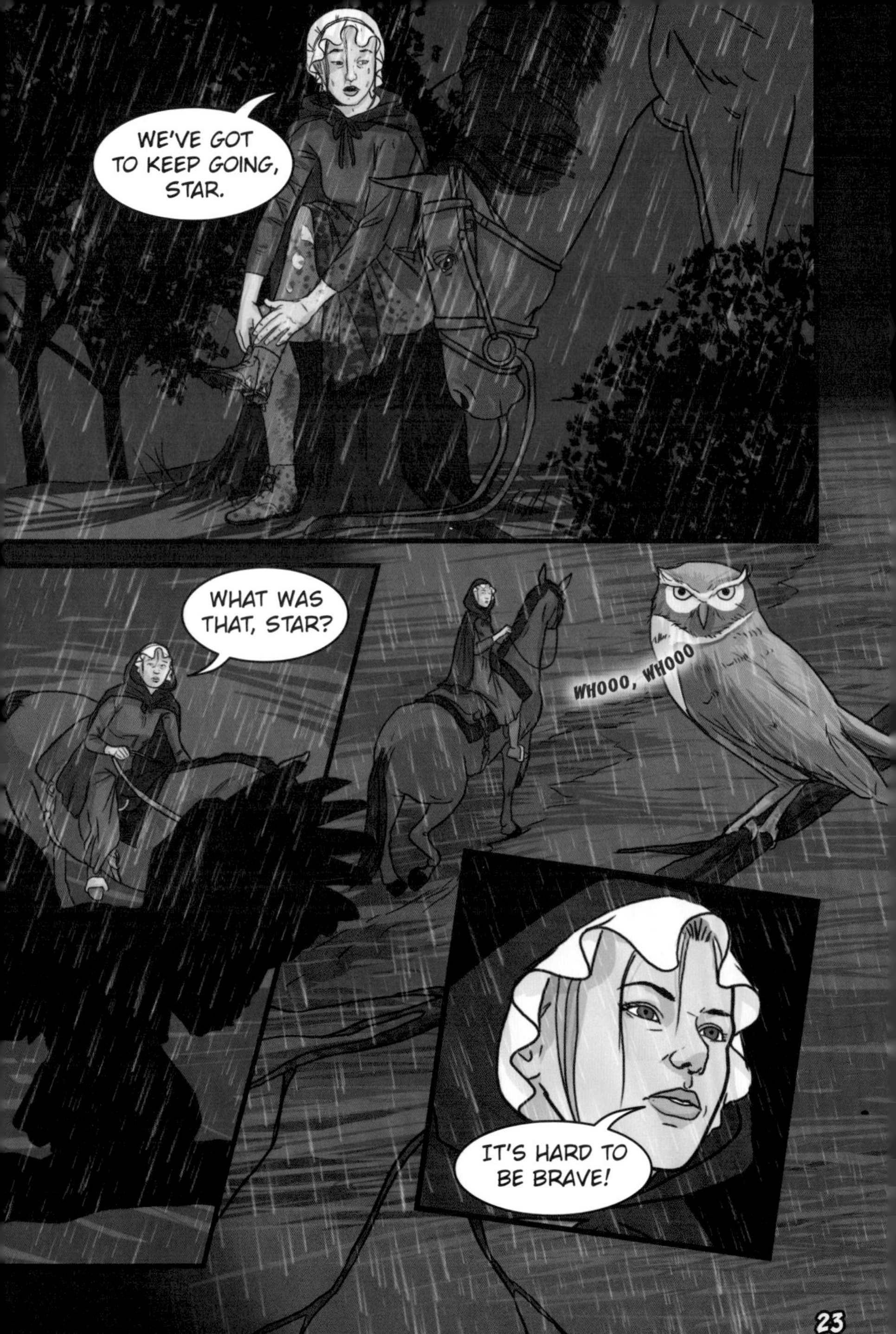
WE'VE GOT TO KEEP GOING, STAR.
WHAT WAS THAT, STAR?
WHOOO, WHOOO
IT'S HARD TO BE BRAVE!

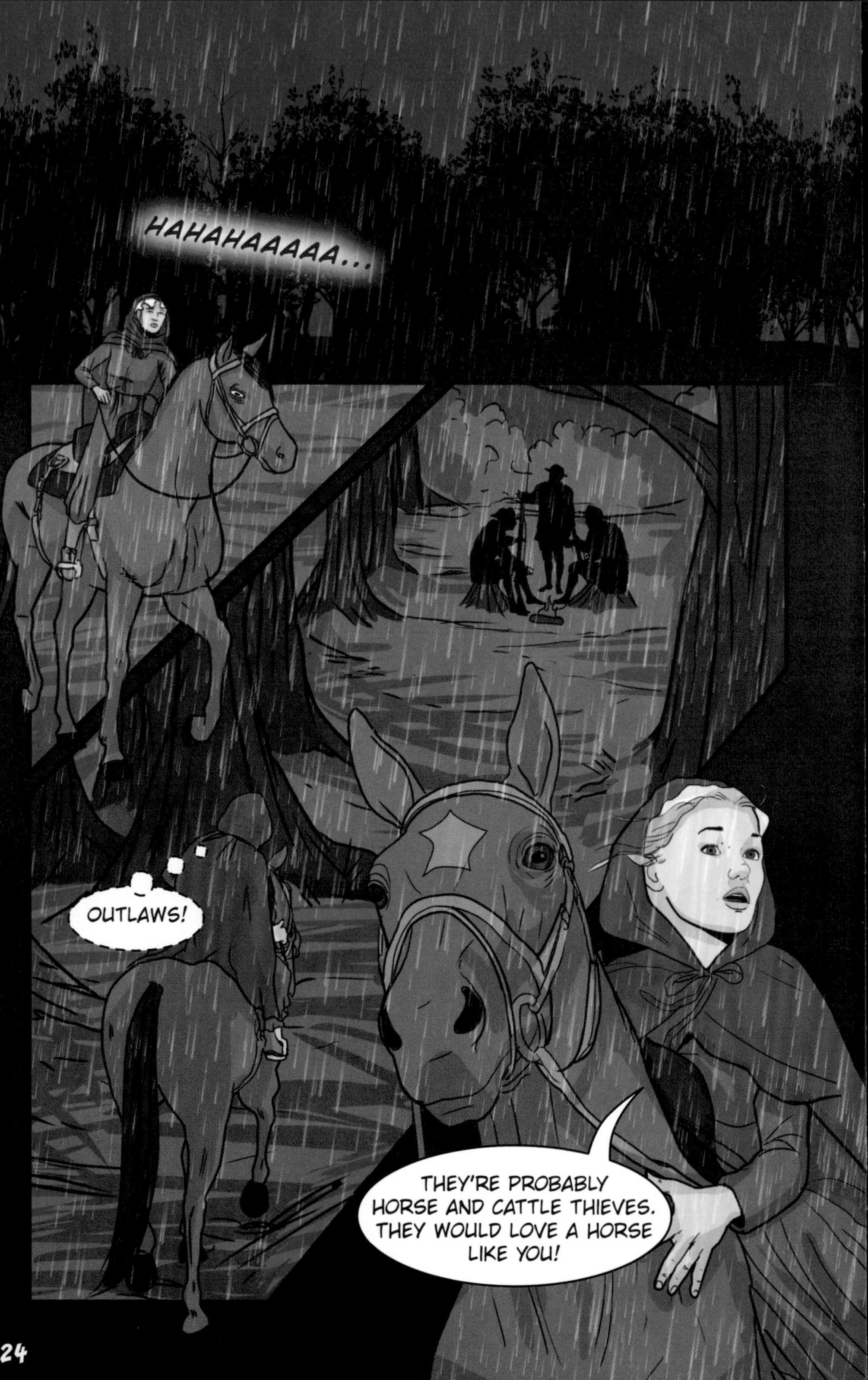
HAHAHAAAAA...
OUTLAWS!
THEY'RE PROBABLY HORSE AND CATTLE THIEVES. THEY WOULD LOVE A HORSE LIKE YOU!

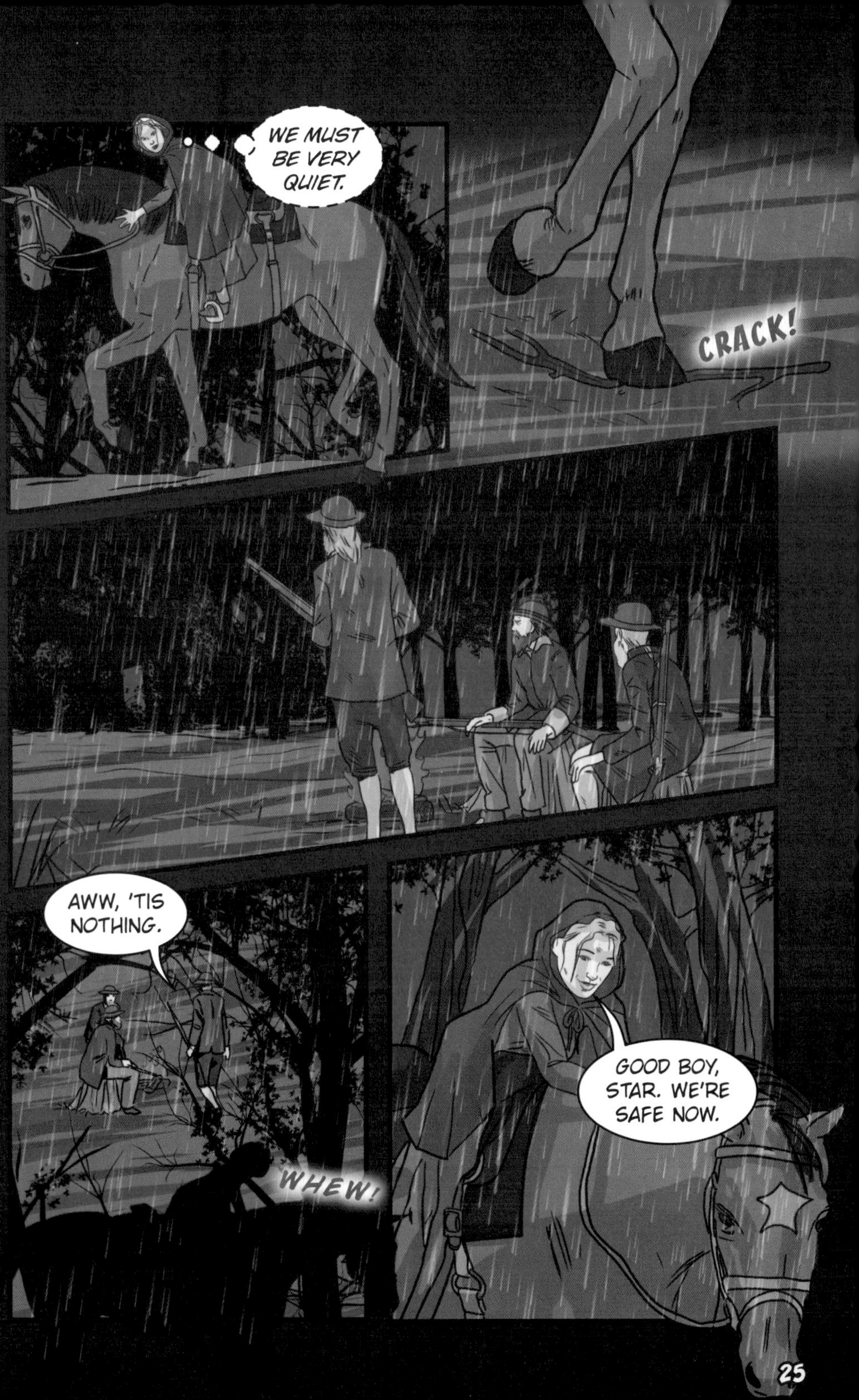
WE MUST BE VERY QUIET.
CRACK!
AWW, 'TIS NOTHING.
WHEW!
GOOD BOY, STAR. WE'RE SAFE NOW.

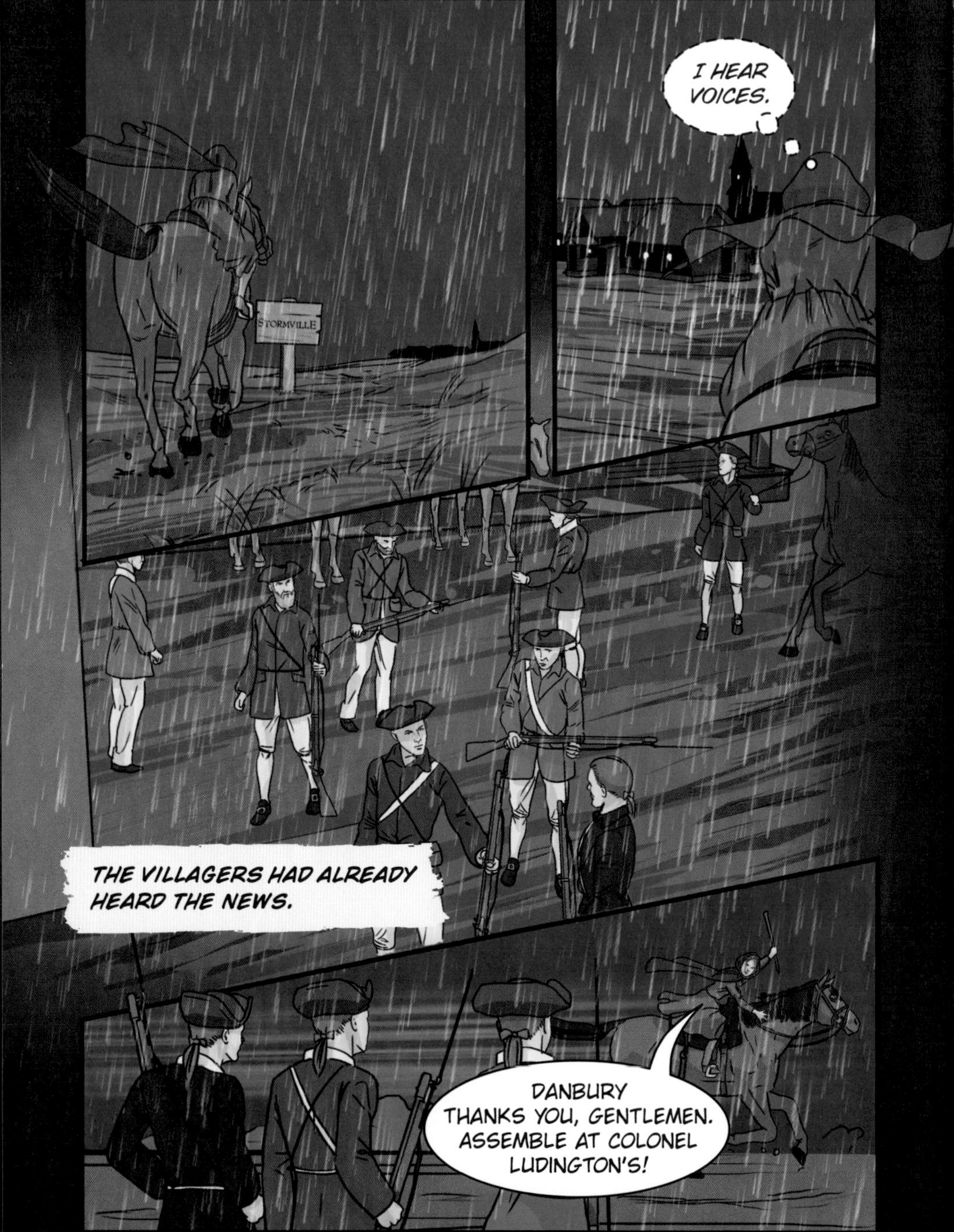
STORMVILLE
I HEAR VOICES.
THE VILLAGERS HAD ALREADY HEARD THE NEWS.
DANBURY THANKS YOU, GENTLEMEN. ASSEMBLE AT COLONEL LUDINGTON'S!

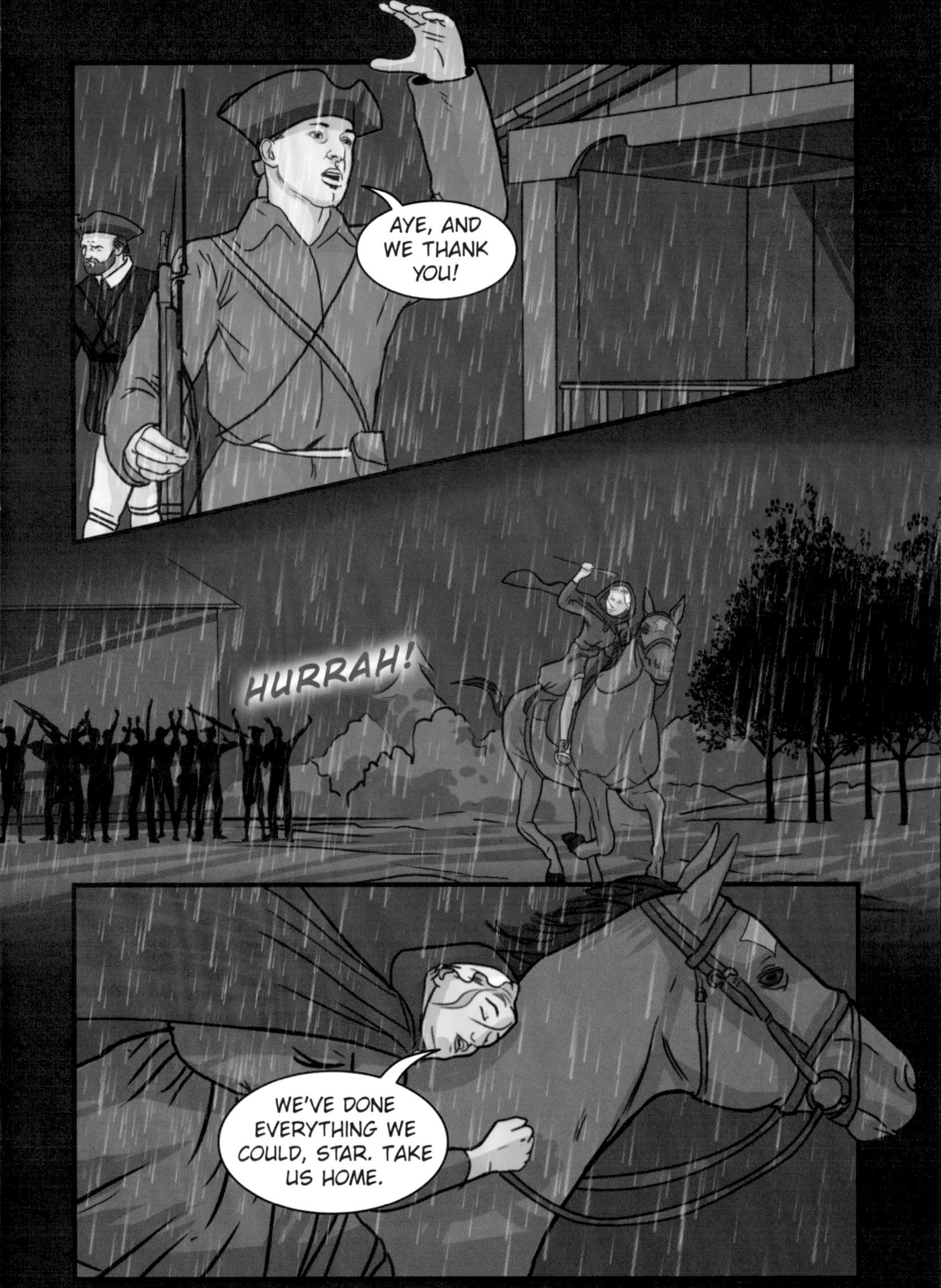
AYE, AND WE THANK YOU!
HURRAH!
WE'VE DONE EVERYTHING WE COULD, STAR. TAKE US HOME.

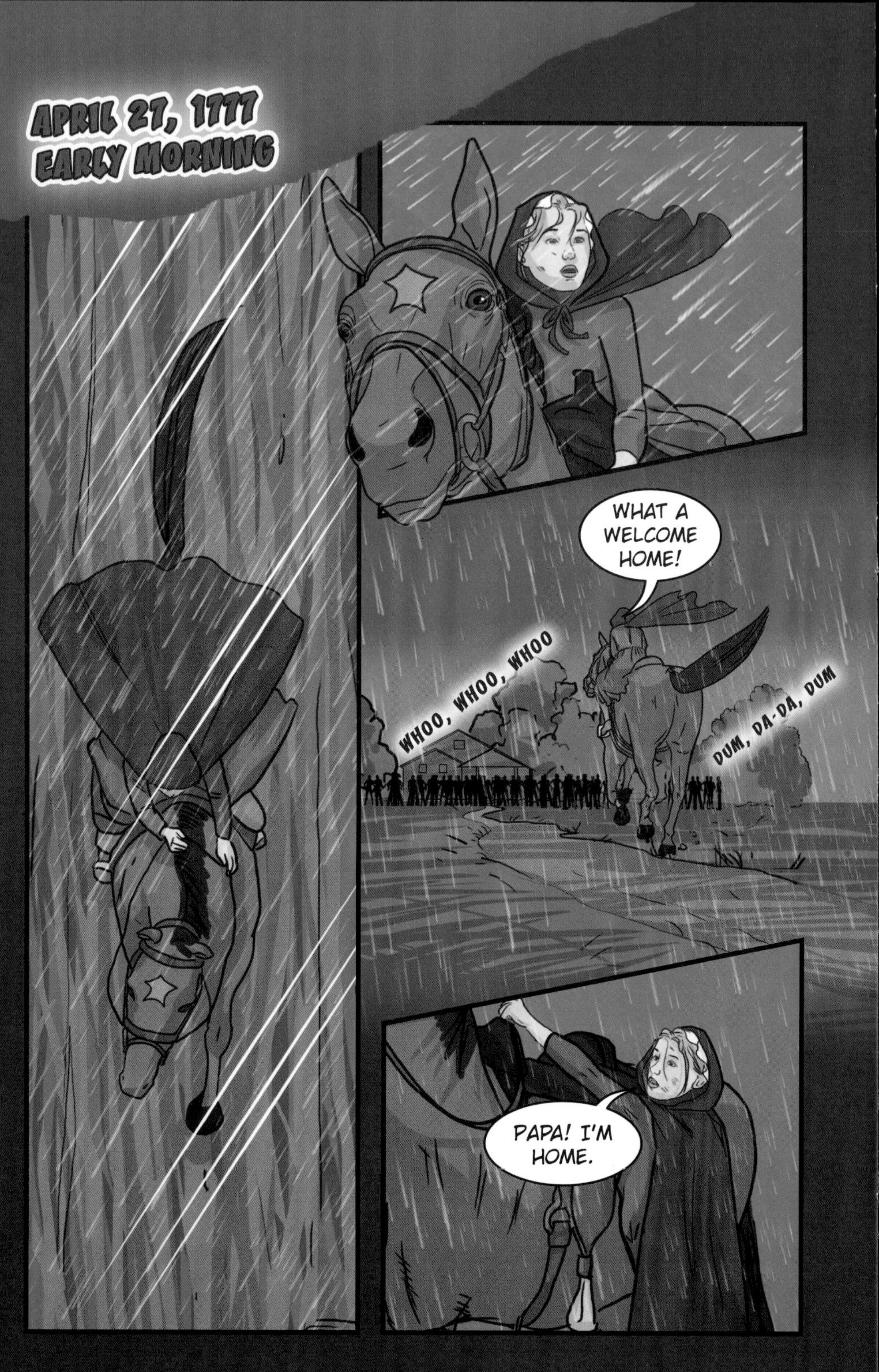
APRIL 27, 1777
EARLY MORNING
WHAT A WELCOME HOME!
WHOO, WHOO, WHOO
DUM, DA-DA, DUM
PAPA! I'M HOME.

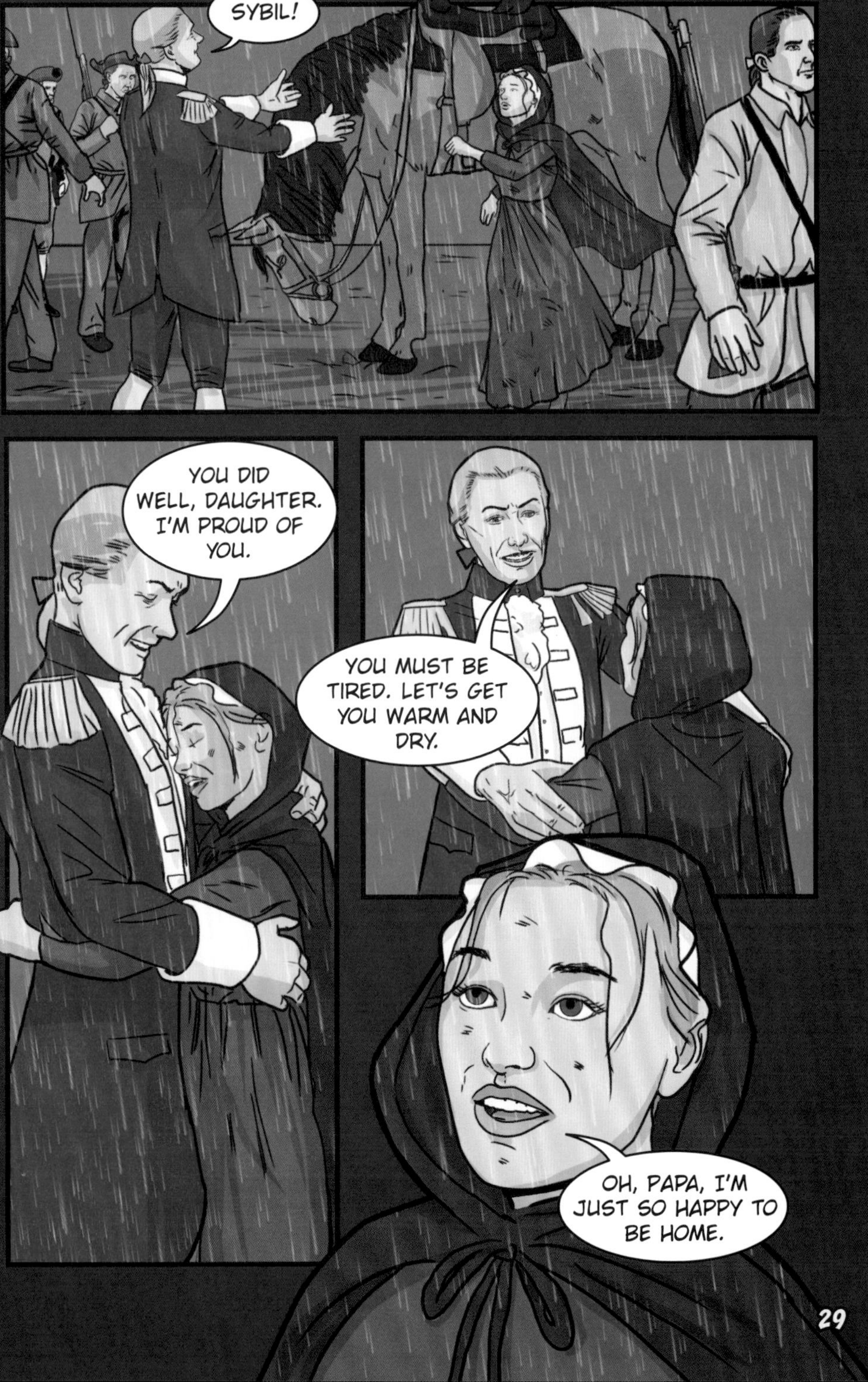
SYBIL!
YOU DID WELL, DAUGHTER. I'M PROUD OF YOU.
YOU MUST BE TIRED. LET'S GET YOU WARM AND DRY.
OH, PAPA, I'M JUST SO HAPPY TO BE HOME.

AFTERWORD

THAT DAY, WHILE SYBIL SLEPT, MILITIA FROM NEW YORK AND CONNECTICUT MARCHED TO MEET THE BRITISH. THE AMERICANS WERE OUTNUMBERED, BUT THE BRITISH WERE TAKEN BY SURPRISE. THROUGHOUT APRIL 27 AND 28, THE MILITIA CHASED THE BRITISH AS THEY TRIED TO RETURN TO THEIR SHIPS. THE BRITISH SAILED AWAY, HAVING DONE MUCH DAMAGE. BUT THEY HAD BEEN STOPPED FROM OCCUPYING THE AREA, AND THEY NEVER ATTEMPTED A SIMILAR RAID.

THE AMERICANS WON THE WAR IN 1783. A YEAR LATER, SYBIL MARRIED EDMOND OGDEN. THEY HAD ONE SON, HENRY, NAMED FOR COLONEL LUDINGTON. SYBIL LIVED TO BE 78 YEARS OLD.

LIKE MANY WOMEN IN HISTORY, SYBIL'S CONTRIBUTION WAS ALMOST FORGOTTEN. BUT, IN 1907, TWO OF HER GREAT-GREAT-GRANDCHILDREN PUBLISHED A BOOK ABOUT HER HEROISM. MORE AND MORE PEOPLE HEARD OF HER STORY AND WERE INSPIRED BY IT.

IN CARMEL, NEW YORK, ON THE PATH OF SYBIL'S RIDE, IS A BIG STATUE OF SYBIL AND STAR. THE STATUE REMINDS US OF ALL THE FORGOTTEN HEROES, BOTH WOMEN AND MEN, WHOSE BRAVERY SHAPED OUR COUNTRY'S HISTORY.

FURTHER READING AND WEBSITES

AMERICA'S STORY FROM AMERICA'S LIBRARY: REVOLUTIONARY PERIOD
HTTP://WWW.AMERICASLIBRARY.GOV/JB/REVOLUT/JB_REVOLUT_SUBJ
.HTML

CATEL, PATRICK. *THE HOME FRONT OF THE REVOLUTIONARY WAR*. NEW
YORK: HEINEMANN INFOSEARCH, 2010.

DACQUINO, VINCENT T. *SYBIL LUDINGTON: DISCOVERING THE LIFE OF
A REVOLUTIONARY WAR HERO*. FLEISCHMANNS, NY: PURPLE MOUNTAIN
PRESS, 2008.

EARLY AMERICA'S MINUTE-MEN
HTTP://WWW.EARLYAMERICA.COM/EARLYAMERICA/BOOKMARKS/MINUTEMEN/

FIGLEY, MARTY RHODES. *JOHN GREENWOOD'S JOURNEY TO BUNKER
HILL*. MINNEAPOLIS: MILLBROOK PRESS, 2011.

FIGLEY, MARTY RHODES. *THE PRISON-SHIP ADVENTURE OF JAMES
FORTEN, REVOLUTIONARY WAR CAPTIVE*. MINNEAPOLIS: GRAPHIC
UNIVERSE, 2011.

MICKLOS, JOHN, JR. *THE BRAVE WOMEN AND CHILDREN OF THE
AMERICAN REVOLUTION*. BERKELEY HEIGHTS, NJ: ENSLOW ELEMENTARY,
2009.

MILLER, BRANDON MARIE. *GROWING UP IN REVOLUTION AND THE NEW
NATION 1775–1800*. MINNEAPOLIS: LERNER PUBLICATIONS COMPANY, 2003.

ROOP, PETER, AND CONNIE ROOP. *THE TOP-SECRET ADVENTURE OF JOHN
DARRAGH, REVOLUTIONARY WAR SPY*. MINNEAPOLIS: GRAPHIC UNIVERSE,
2011.

SOCIAL STUDIES FOR KIDS: THE AMERICAN REVOLUTIONARY WAR
HTTP://WWW.SOCIALSTUDIESFORKIDS.COM/ARTICLES/USHISTORY/
REVOLUTIONARYWAR1.HTM

ABOUT THE AUTHOR

MARSHA AMSTEL NOT ONLY WRITES BOOKS FOR CHILDREN, SHE IS A FAMILY THERAPIST IN PUTNAM VALLEY, NEW YORK. IN HER SPARE TIME, SHE ENJOYS HIKING, KAYAKING, AND SNOWSHOEING, ALL WITHIN A FEW MILES OF THE ROUTE OF SYBIL'S MIDNIGHT RIDE.

ABOUT THE ADAPTER

AMANDA DOERING TOURVILLE HAS WRITTEN MORE THAN FORTY BOOKS FOR CHILDREN. SHE IS GREATLY HONORED TO WRITE FOR YOUNG PEOPLE AND HOPES THAT THEY WILL LEARN TO LOVE READING AND LEARNING AS MUCH AS SHE DOES. WHEN NOT WRITING, TOURVILLE ENJOYS TRAVELING, PHOTOGRAPHY, AND HIKING. SHE LIVES IN MINNESOTA WITH HER HUSBAND AND GUINEA PIG.

ABOUT THE ILLUSTRATORS

TED HAMMOND IS A CANADIAN ARTIST, LIVING AND WORKING JUST OUTSIDE OF TORONTO. HAMMOND HAS CREATED ARTWORK FOR EVERYTHING FROM FANTASY AND COMIC-BOOK ART TO CHILDREN'S MAGAZINES, POSTERS, AND BOOK ILLUSTRATION.

RICHARD PIMENTEL CARBAJAL HAS A BROAD SPECTRUM OF ILLUSTRATIVE SPECIALTIES. HIS BACKGROUND HAS FOCUSED ON LARGE-SCALE INSTALLATIONS AND SCENERY. CARBAJAL RECENTLY HAS EXPANDED INTO THE BOOK PUBLISHING AND ADVERTISING MARKETS.

Text copyright © 2012 by Marsha Amstel
Illustrations © 2012 by Lerner Publishing Group, Inc.

Graphic Universe™ is a trademark of Lerner Publishing Group, Inc.

Graphic Universe™
A division of Lerner Publishing Group, Inc.
241 First Avenue North
Minneapolis, MN 55401 U.S.A.

Website address: www.lernerbooks.com

Amstel, Marsha
    The horse-riding adventure of Sybil Ludington, Revolutionary War messenger / by Marsha Amstel ; adapted by Amanda Doering Tourville ; illustrated by Ted Hammond and Richard Carbajal.
        p.   cm. — (History's kid heroes)
    Summary: In 1777, on a cold and stormy night in the New York Colony, sixteen-year-old Sybil Ludington makes a dangerous and difficult ride to warn the local militiamen that the British Army is looting and burning nearby Danbury, Connecticut.
    Includes bibliographical references.
    ISBN: 978–0–7613–6181–7 (lib. bdg. : alk. paper)
    1. Ludington, Sybil, b. 1761—Juvenile fiction. 2. United States—History—Revolution, 1775–1783—Juvenile fiction. 3. Danbury (Conn.)—History—Burning by the British, 1777—Juvenile fiction. 4. Graphic novels. [1. Graphic novels. 2. Ludington, Sybil, b. 1761—Fiction. 3. United States—History—Revolution, 1775–1783—Fiction. 4. Danbury (Conn.)—History—Burning by the British, 1777—Fiction.] I. Tourville, Amanda Doering. II. Hammond, Ted, ill. III. Carbajal, Richard, ill. IV. Title.
PZ7.7.T68Hor 2012
973.3'33—dc22   2010035205